"十三五"国家重点出版规划项目

李白诗歌全集英译

A Complete Edition of Pai Li's Poems in Chinese and English
With Annotations

赵彦春 译·注

Translated and Annotated by Yanchun Chao

第七卷

Volume VII

上海大学出版社

·上海·

卷七

目 录
Contents

1467　**古近体诗三十六首**
Old-new Rhythmic Poetry, 36 Poems

1469　登锦城散花楼
Climbing Flower Tower in Silkton

1471　登峨眉山
Climbing Mt. Brow

1473　大庭库
Broad Hall

1475　登单父陶少府半月台
Climbing Crescent Mound with T'ao, Sheriff of Shanfu

1477　天台晓望
Gazing at Dawn on Mt. Heaven

1479　早望海霞边
Looking at Sea Clouds at Dawn

1481　焦山望松寥山
Looking at Mt. Pine Broad on Mt. Burn

1482　杜陵绝句
A Quatrain at Mt. Birchleaf Pear

1483　登太白峰
Climbing up Mt. Venus

1485　登邯郸洪波台置酒观发兵
Climbing Wave Mound in Hantan to Watch Soldiers at Drill While Drinking Wine

1487	登新平楼	
	Climbing New Peace Tower	
1489	谒老君庙	
	A Visit to Laocius's Fane	
1491	秋日登扬州西灵塔	
	Climbing West Soul Pagoda in Yangchow on an Autumn Day	
1493	登金陵冶城西北谢安墩	
	Climbing Hsieh's Mound Northwest of Forgeton in Gold Hill	
1497	登瓦官阁	
	Climbing to the Attic of Potter Temple	
1499	登梅冈望金陵，赠族侄高座寺僧中孚	
	Climbing Wintersweet Mound to Overlook Gold Hill and Dedicating a Verse to My Nephew, a Monk in High Seat Temple	
1503	登金陵凤凰台	
	Climbing Phoenix Mound in Gold Hill	
1505	望庐山瀑布	
	Gazing at the Mt. Lodge Waterfall	
1509	登庐山五老峰	
	Climbing the Five Old Men Peaks on Mt. Lodge	
1510	江上望皖公山	
	Looking at Mt. Wan from the River	
1512	望黄鹤山	
	Staring at Mt. Yellow Crane	
1514	鹦鹉洲	
	Parrot Shoal	
1516	九日登巴陵置酒望洞庭水军	
	Looking at the Fleet on Lake Cavehall While Drinking at the Pa Hills	
1519	秋登巴陵望洞庭	
	Gazing at Cavehall on the Pa's Mound on an Autumn Day	
1521	与夏十二登岳阳楼	
	On the Hillshine Tower with Hsia Twelve	
1522	登巴陵开元寺西阁赠衡岳僧方外	
	Dedication to Monk Outworld in West Hall of All begun Temple on the Pa's Mound	

1524		与贾至舍人于龙兴寺剪落梧桐枝望灉湖 Looking at Lake Rush with Chih Chia, Scribe of Privy Council, at Dragonrise Temple, Holding a Phoenix Tree Spray
1526		挂席江上待月有怀 Setting Sail and Waiting for Luna
1527		金陵望汉江 Gazing at the Han River from Gold Hill
1529		秋登宣城谢朓北楼 An Autumn Afternoon on the North Tower Built by T'iao Hsieh in Hsuan
1531		望天门山 Watching Mt. Skygate
1532		望木瓜山 Gazing at Mt. Pawpaw
1533		登敬亭北二小山,余时送客,逢崔侍御,并登此地 Meeting Ts'ui, the Royal Servant, While Seeing Off My Guest and Climbing Two Small Hills North of Mt. Chingt'ing with Him
1535		过崔八丈水亭 Seeing Old Ts'ui Eight at Riverine Pavilion
1536		登广武古战场怀古 Reminiscing the Past in Broad Mars Battlefield

1539 古近体诗五十八首
Old-new Rhythmic Poetry, 58 Poems

1541		安州应城玉女汤作 The Fairy Hotspring in Ying, Peaceton
1544		之广陵宿常二南郭幽居 Putting Up for the Night in Ch'ang Two's Quiet Abode in Broadridge
1546		夜下征虏亭 Beat Foe Bower Under Night
1547		下途归石门旧居 Returning to the Old Abode at Stone Gate

1551	客中作	
	Away from Home	
1552	太原早秋	
	Early Autumn in Great Plain	
1553	奔亡道中五首	
	Fleeing on the Way, Five Poems	
1560	郢门秋怀	
	Touched by Autumn in Ying Gate	
1562	至鸭栏驿上白马矶赠裴侍御	
	To P'ei, the Royal Servant, at White Horse Stack at Duck Pen Post	
1564	荆门浮舟望蜀江	
	Looking at the Shu River While Boating in Chastegate	
1566	上三峡	
	Rowing in Three Gorges	
1567	自巴东舟行经瞿唐峡登巫山最高峰晚还题壁	
	Boating from East Pa via Big Pond Gorge, Climbing Mt. Witch and Writing an Inscription on a Cliff When Coming Back at Dusk	
1570	早发白帝城	
	Early Departure from Whitegod	
1571	秋下荆门	
	Leaving Shu for Mt. Chastegate in Autumn	
1572	江行寄远	
	To My Friend When I Row on the River	
1573	宿五松山下荀媪家	
	Putting Up at Mother Hsun's at the Foot of Mt. Five Pines	
1575	下泾县陵阳溪至涩滩	
	From the Ridgeshine Stream in Ching County to Hard Sands	
1576	下陵阳沿高溪三门六刺滩	
	From Ridgeshine to Three Gates and Six Pricks on the High Stream	
1577	夜泊黄山闻殷十四吴吟	
	Hearing Wu Fourteen Chanting a Song of Wu When I Put Up for the Night at Mt. Yellow	

1579	宿鰕湖	
	Put Up for the Night on Lake Shrimp	
1581	西施	
	West Maid	
1583	王右军	
	Right General Wang	
1585	上元夫人	
	Lady Up	
1587	苏台览古	
	Visiting Kusu Mound	
1588	越中览古	
	Visiting the Relics in Yüeh	
1589	商山四皓	
	The Four Old Men at Mt. Shang	
1591	过四皓墓	
	The Tombs of the Four Old Men	
1593	岘山怀古	
	Visiting an Old Sight on Mt. Steep	
1595	苏武	
	Wu Su	
1597	经下邳圯桥怀张子房	
	Thinking of Tsefang on the Bridge in Hsiap'i	
1599	金陵三首	
	Gold Hill, Three Poems	
1603	秋夜板桥浦泛月独酌怀谢朓	
	Drinking and Missing T'iao Hsieh in Slab Bridge Shore on an Autumn Night	
1605	过彭蠡湖	
	A Visit to P'oshine Lake	
1607	入彭蠡,经松门观石镜,缅怀谢康乐,题诗书游览之志	
	Looking into Stone Mirror on Mt. Pinegate on My Way to P'oshine, Reminiscing Lord Glee and Writing a Verse to Express My Will	
1610	庐江主人妇	
	A Wife in Lodgeriver	

1611	陪宋中丞武昌夜饮怀古
	Drinking at Night with Magistrate Sung to Reminisce the Past in Mightboom
1613	望鹦鹉洲怀祢衡
	Missing Scale Mi While Gazing at Parrot Shoal
1615	宿巫山下
	Putting Up for the Night Below Mt. Witch
1617	金陵白杨十字巷
	White Poplar Crossroads Lane in Gold Hill
1619	谢公亭
	Lord Glee's Kiosk
1621	纪南陵题五松山
	Writing an Inscription on Mt. Five Pines in Southridge
1624	夜泊牛渚怀古
	One Night on Mt. Ox Shoal
1625	姑孰溪
	The Kushu Stream
1626	丹阳湖
	Lake Redshine
1627	谢公宅
	Lord Glee's House
1629	凌歊台
	Rising Mound
1631	桓公井
	Lord Pillar's Well
1632	慈姥竹
	Loving Granny's Bamboo
1634	望夫山
	Mt. O Come Hubby
1635	牛渚矶
	Ox Shoal Boulder
1636	灵墟山
	Mt. Soul's Wasteland

| 1637 | 天门山 |
| | Mt. Skygate |

| 1639 | **古近体诗四十七首** |
| | Old-new Rhythmic Poetry, 47 Poems |

| 1641 | 与元丹丘方城寺谈玄作 |
| | Talking about Sutra with Redknoll Yüan in Squareton Temple |

| 1643 | 寻高凤石门山中元丹丘 |
| | Visiting Redknoll Yüan in Hiphoenix's Mt. Stonegate |

| 1645 | 安州般若寺水阁纳凉，喜遇薛员外义 |
| | Enjoying the Cool in Prajna Temple in Peaceton, Where I Meet Worth Hsüeh, a Ministry Councillor |

| 1647 | 鲁中都东楼醉起作 |
| | Written on East Tower When Drunk in Midtown of Lu |

| 1648 | 对酒醉题屈突明府厅 |
| | Writing an Inscription for Magistrate Ch'ut'u's Hall When Drunk |

| 1649 | 月下独酌四首 |
| | Drinking Alone Under the Moon, Four Poems |

| 1657 | 春归终南山松龛旧隐 |
| | Retiring to the Old Abode of Pine Shrine in the South Hill in Spring |

| 1659 | 冬夜醉宿龙门觉起言志 |
| | Putting Up for the Night at Dragongate When Drunk on a Winter Night and Expressing My Will When Waking Up |

| 1662 | 寻山僧不遇作 |
| | Written When Failing to See the Monk |

| 1664 | 过汪氏别业二首 |
| | In Wang's Villa, Two Poems |

| 1668 | 待酒不至 |
| | Drinking till Late |

| 1669 | 独酌 |
| | Drinking Alone |

1671	友人会宿
	Staying with My Friend One Night
1672	春日独酌二首
	Drinking Alone on a Spring Day, Two Poems
1675	金陵江上遇蓬池隐者
	Meeting Thistle Pond Hermit on the Goldhill River
1678	月夜听卢子顺弹琴
	Listening to Tseshun Lu Playing the Zither on a Moonlit Night
1680	清溪半夜闻笛
	Hearing a Flute Tune by the Wu Stream at Midnight
1681	日夕山中忽然有怀
	Inspired in the Hills at Dusk
1683	夏日山中
	In the Hills on a Summer's Day
1684	山中与幽人对酌
	Drinking with a Hermit 'mid Mountain Blooms
1685	春日醉起言志
	Standing Up to Express Myself While Drunk
1687	庐山东林寺夜怀
	A Night in Eastwood Temple on Mt. Lodge
1689	寻雍尊师隐居
	Looking for Master Reverent in Hiding
1690	与史郎中钦听黄鹤楼上吹笛
	Listening to a Flute Play with Shih, the Royal Guard, in Yellow Crane Tower
1691	对酒
	Drinking Wine with a Friend
1693	醉题王汉阳厅
	Writing an Inscription for Magistrate Wang's Hall
1694	嘲王历阳不肯饮酒
	Laughing at Wang, Magistrate of Leeshine, Who Does Not Drink Wine
1696	独坐敬亭山
	Sitting Alone Before Mt. Chingt'ing

1697	自遣	
	Drinking to Myself	
1698	访戴天山道士不遇	
	Failing to See the Monk on Mt. Skywear	
1700	秋日与张少府、楚城韦公藏书高斋作	
	Staying with Sheriff Chang and Wei, Magistrate of Ch'u, in the Latter's Library on an Autumn Day	
1702	秋夜独坐怀故山	
	Reminiscing the Old Hill When Sitting Alone on an Autumn Night	
1704	忆崔郎中宗之游南阳遗吾孔子琴抚之潸然感旧	
	Reminiscing Tsungchih Ts'ui, the Royal Guard, Touring Southshine, and Crying over the Lute He Left to Me	
1707	忆东山二首	
	Recollection of the East Hills, Two Poems	
1709	望月有怀	
	Stirred When Looking at the Moon	
1710	对酒忆贺监二首(并序)	
	Drinking and Reminiscing Mr. Ho, Two Poems with an Introduction	
1713	重忆一首	
	Reminiscing the Past	
1714	春滞沅湘有怀山中	
	Feeling Touched in the Hills When Kept at Bay in the Yüan-Hsiang Area in Spring	
1716	落日忆山中	
	Reminiscing the Hills at Sunset	
1717	忆秋浦桃花旧游,时窜夜郎	
	Reminiscing My Tour in Autumn Shore While Exiled to Nightboy	

古近体诗三十六首
Old-new Rhythmic Poetry, 36 Poems

登锦城散花楼

日照锦城头，
朝光散花楼。
金窗夹绣户，
珠箔悬银钩。
飞梯绿云中，
极目散我忧。
暮雨向三峡，
春江绕双流。
今来一登望，
如上九天游。

Climbing Flower Tower in Silkton

The sun sheds light to Silkton bright,
And Flower Tower basks in morning light.
The gold window with a screen furled,
The jade hook on the curtain pearled.
A ladder flies into green air;
The sight disperses all my care.
To Three Gorges comes the dusk rain;
A spring stream flows into Flows Twain.
Now on the tower I cast my eyes
As if I'm touring the blue skies.

* Silkton: the ancient name for Ch'engtu for it was a town famous for silk.
* screen: a curtain which separates or cuts off, shelters or protects as a light partition, a

common image in Chinese literature. A poem in *The Book of Songs* reads like this: "You wait for me before the screen; / Your hat-rings white do tinkle clean, / And your rubies brilliantly sheen."

* Three Gorges: referring to the three gorges of the Long River, including Big Pond Gorge, Witch Gorge, and Westridge Gorge, a set of spectacular gorges formed where the Long River cuts its way through the formidable Witch Mountains, forming a three-hundred-kilometer stretch of very narrow canyons.
* Flows Twain: referring to two canals in the areas under Silkton. Two main canals were dug under the governance of Ping Li (cir. 302 B.C.– 235 B.C.) in the plains of Silkton to irrigate the fields in his prefecture.

登 峨 眉 山

蜀国多仙山，
峨眉邈难匹。
周流试登览，
绝怪安可悉？
青冥倚天开，
彩错疑画出。
泠然紫霞赏，
果得锦囊术。
云间吟琼箫，
石上弄宝瑟。
平生有微尚，
欢笑自此毕。
烟容如在颜，
尘累忽相失。
倘逢骑羊子，
携手凌白日。

Climbing Mt. Brow

In Shu abound fairy hills fair,
But they can't with Mt. Brow compare.
Now you can climb up and climb high;
All faeries rush on to your eye.
On the skyline the green hills line;
The colors like a painting shine.
Atop the peak hued clouds you'll see,

And an immortal you can be.
Amid the clouds I play the flute;
Upon the stone you pluck the lute.
The Wordist group I would join in,
Smiling, something new to begin.
There glamour appears on my face;
The dust world goes away apace.
Into a saint if I could run;
Hand in hand we'd fly to the sun.

* Mt. Brow: one of the four Buddhist mountains, located in today's Ssuch'uan Province, named for its elegant brow-shaped silhouette viewed from a distance.
* Shu: one of the earliest kingdoms in China, founded by Silkworm according to legend. In the Three Kingdoms period, a new Shu was established by Pei Liu, hence one of the three kingdoms in that period.
* Wordist: one who believes in and practices the Word, the ultimate force in anything and the Creator of all things. In the T'ang dynasty, an age of proselytism, while Confucianism remained the guiding principle of state and social morality, Wordism had gathered an incrustation of mythology and superstition and was fast winning a following of both the court and the common people. Laocius, the founder, was claimed by the reigning dynasty as its remote progenitor and was honored with an imperial title, Emperor Dark One.

大 庭 库

朝登大庭库，
云物何苍然！
莫辨陈郑火，
空霾邹鲁烟。
我来寻梓慎，
观化入寥天。
古木翔气多，
松风如五弦。
帝图终冥没，
叹息满山川。

Broad Hall

The morn sees me climb to Broad Hall;
The disaster seen does scare all!
In Ch'en or Cheng? One can't discern;
Tsou and Lu, the fire would all burn.
I'll find the one who can tell why
And tell what will fall from the sky.
The olden wood a north wind brings;
The pine needles pluck the lute strings.
The emperor's blueprints now die;
All hills and rills let out a sigh.

* Broad Hall: located in today's Chockfull (Ch'üfu) County, Shant'ung Province.
* In Ch'en or Cheng: According to records, there was a fire so big that one could not tell

from where it spread.
* Tsou and Lu: two vassal states. Tsou was the birthplace of Mencius, and Lu of Confucius.

登单父陶少府半月台

陶公有逸兴，
不与常人俱。
筑台像半月，
迥向高城隅。
置酒望白云，
商飙起寒梧。
秋山入远海，
桑柘罗平芜。
水色渌且明，
令人思镜湖。
终当过江去，
爱此暂踟蹰。

Climbing Crescent Mound with T'ao, Sheriff of Shanfu

You're graceful with an easy mind,
So different from the common kind.
Much like the crescent, half a ball,
The mound you built greets the high wall.
Let's set wine to look at clouds now;
From phoenix trees there blows a sough.
The autumn hills roll to the sea;
The mulberries up line tree by tree.
The water like blue jade does blink;
Of Lake Mirror in Yüeh I think.

Across the river we should go;
Bewitched here, I pace to and fro.

* Shanfu: a county in present-day Shantung, so named because Father Shan (Shanfu) lived here and declined Lord Mound's offer of the throne.
* Lake Mirror: a large reservoir built in the Han dynasty, higher than the fields and the fields higher than the sea, 310 li in circumference.
* Yüeh: an ancient vassal state of Chough, implying a vague area of southern lands.

天 台 晓 望

天台邻四明,
华顶高百越。
门标赤城霞,
楼栖沧岛月。
凭危一登览,
直下见溟渤。
云垂大鹏翻,
波动巨鳌没。
风涛尚汹涌,
神怪何翕忽?
观奇迹足倪,
好道心不歇。
攀条摘朱实,
服药炼真骨。
安得生羽翰?
千秋卧蓬阙。

Gazing at Dawn on Mt. Heaven

Mt. Heaven is near Mt. Four Bright;
In Yüeh, the highest is its height.
The red crags to Red Town do smile;
The moon will perch on the Blue Isle.
I climb up 'nd on the rail rely
To see waves down below surge high.
Clouds like giant rocs turn all around;

Waves like huge whales rise and get drowned.
To chase high wind the breakers surge;
Deities and monsters there emerge.
For all scenes here, saints I can't find;
I cannot settle down my mind.
Pick berries from the twigs I must
To make cure-all for bones robust.
How could I grow plumes? I aspire;
O'er Fairy Isle I would fly higher.

* Mt. Heaven: alias Mt. Heaven Terrace, a mountain in Chechiang Province.
* Mt. Four Bright: a mountain in Chechiang Province, standing opposite to Mt. Heaven Terrace.
* Yüeh: the State of Yüeh (2032 B.C.- 222 B.C.), a vassal state under Hsia, Shang and Chough in Southeast China in the Spring and Autumn period. As a regime, it was first founded by Nothing Left (Wuyü), King Young Health (Shaok'ang) of Hsia' son born of a concubine.
* Red Town: Mt. Red Town, a mountain in Chechiang Province.
* the moon: the planet of the earth, which appears at night and gives off shining silvery light, an image of purity and solitude in Chinese culture.
* the Blue Isle: unidentified. It can be understood as an isle in the ocean.
* roc: a legendary enormous powerful bird of prey. In Chinese mythology, it was transformed from a fish in North Sea. *Sir Lush* reads like this: There in North Sea is a fish called Minnow, whose body spans about a thousand miles. When transformed into a bird, it is called Roc, whose back spans about a thousand miles. With a burst of vigor, it flies up, whose wings are like clouds hemming the sky. This bird, skimming tides, flies to South Sea. And this South Sea is called the Pool of Heaven.
* whale: a cetaceous mammal of fish-like form, especially one of the larger pelagic species, as distinguished from dolphins and porpoises. Whales have the fore limbs developed as broad flattened paddles, hind limbs absent, and a thick layer of fat or blubber immediately beneath the skin. A whale is a symbol of great ambition, fortitude and uniqueness.
* Fairy Isle: an imaginary ideal place where one can live happily forever.

早望海霞边

四明三千里，
朝起赤城霞。
日出红光散，
分辉照雪崖。
一餐咽琼液，
五内发金沙。
举手何所待？
青龙白虎车。

Looking at Sea Clouds at Dawn

One thousand miles rolls Mt. Four Bright;
You'd rise early for Red Town light.
The sun gives off red sparkling streaks
That brighten up the snow-capped peaks.
With one swallow of nectar canned,
The vitals feel filled with gold sand.
Who are you waving your hand to?
The cart drawn by the dragon blue.

* Mt. Four Bright: a mountain in today's Chechiang Province, standing opposite to Mt. Heaven Terrace.
* Red Town: Mt. Red Town, a mountain in today's Chechiang Province.
* nectar: in Chinese and Greek mythologies, the drink of the gods or fairies, and in botany, the saccharine substance secreted by some plants and forming the base of natural honey.

* dragon: a fabulous serpent-like giant winged animal that can change its girth and length, a totem of the Chinese nation, a symbol of benevolence and sovereignty in Chinese culture.

焦山望松寥山

石壁望松寥，
宛然在碧霄。
安得五彩虹，
驾天作长桥。
仙人如爱我，
举手来相招。

Looking at Mt. Pine Broad on Mt. Burn

Upon the cliff I look at Pine Broad,
As if over blue clouds I soared.
How can I a rainbow come by
As a long bridge to reach the sky?
Oh, Fairy, if you show me love,
You can wave to me from above.

* Mt. Pine Broad: also known as Sea Gate, an islet located at the estuary of the Yangtze River, faced with Mt. Burn on the mainland. Due to the silting of the Yangtze River the two hills are now joined together.
* Mt. Burn: located in today's Chenchiang, opposite Mt. Pine Broad, so named because a hermit called Burn First once lived here.

杜 陵 绝 句

南登杜陵上,
北望五陵间。
秋水明落日,
流光灭远山。

A Quatrain at Mt. Birchleaf Pear

From south I climb up Birchleaf Pear;
To north I gaze at Mt. Five there.
The chill stream gilds the setting sun;
The freaks of light to far hills run.

* Birchleaf Pear: Mt. Birchleaf Pear, located in today's Hsi-an, Sha'anhsi Province.
* Mt. Five: referring to the mausoleums of five emperors of T'ang, which later became a prosperous area that notable families resided.

登太白峰

西上太白峰,
夕阳穷登攀。
太白与我语,
为我开天关。
愿乘泠风去,
直出浮云间。
举手可近月,
前行若无山。
一别武功去,
何时复更还?

Climbing up Mt. Venus

I climb up Mt. Venus from west;
At dusk I arrive at the crest.
Yeah? Venus speaks to me, alas!
For me it opens Heaven Pass.
I'd ride a cold breeze to go there,
To float with white clouds in the air.
My hand raised, I can fetch moon beams;
There're no mountains ahead it seems.
I'll leave Merit and go away;
When can I come back, o which day?

* Mt. Venus: the highest peak of Ch'in Ridge and also the highest peak in China east of Blue Sea-Tibetan Plateau, a Wordist sanctuary, known for its height, coldness,

dangerousness, strangeness and bountifulness.
* Heaven Pass: a pass leading to Heaven the poet imagined.
* Merit: Mt. Merit, a mountain located on the south of Mt. Venus.

登邯郸洪波台置酒观发兵

我把两赤羽，
来游燕赵间。
天狼正可射，
感激无时闲。
观兵洪波台，
倚剑望玉关。
请缨不系越，
且向燕然山。
风引龙虎旗，
歌钟昔追攀。
击筑落高月，
投壶破愁颜。
遥知百战胜，
定扫鬼方还。

Climbing Wave Mound in Hantan to Watch Soldiers at Drill While Drinking Wine

Of red plumed arrows I take two
And to Yan and Chao I now go.
Right now, the dog star I shoot at;
I'm so inspired, inspired like that.
On Surge Mound I watch soldiers drilled;
And gaze at Jade Gate Pass as willed.
I'll go to war, not in Yüeh stay,
And to Mt. Yanjan make my way.

Against the wind the flags fast wave;
Drum beaten, dangers I will brave.
I pluck the *quin* to lure the moon,
And cast the pot, and sing a croon.
We'll win all battles to attack,
And wipe all Huns ere we come back.

* Hantan: the capital of the State of Chao in the Eastern Chough dynasty, present-day Hantan, Hopei Province.
* Yan and Chao: two ancient vassal states, implying northern region in general.
* Surge Mound: 2.5 kilometers from Hantan in the T'ang dynasty.
* Jade Gate Pass: an important military fort and passage on the Silk Road, built in the Han dynasty, located in the north of today's Tunhuang, Kansu Province. As is recorded, to guard against Hun invasions, Emperor Martial of Han formed alliance with nations in the western regions to initiate the route between east and west, and instituted four sires and built two passes with beacons west of the Yellow River. Fortresses were made from Lingchü to Wine Spring in 111 B.C. and more fortresses made from Wine Spring to Jade Gate.
* Yüeh: an ancient vassal state, implying a vague area of the southern land.
* Mt. Yanjan: a mountain located in present-day Mongolia. It is usually used to imply an enemy with military threat.
* *quin*: an ancient Chinese musical instrument with five strings like a quinton.
* Hun: northern barbaric Asian people or invaders in general, who occupied vast regions from Mongolia to Central Asia in Chinese history, especially during the Han dynasty. They were a headache and a constant menace on China's western and northern borders.

登 新 平 楼

去国登兹楼，
怀归伤暮秋。
天长落日远，
水净寒波流。
秦云起岭树，
胡雁飞沙洲。
苍苍几万里，
目极令人愁。

Climbing New Peace Tower

I climb this tower before I go;
The autumn late adds to my woe.
The sun sets to the skyline vast;
The river cold and calm flows past.
Ch'in's clouds rise o'er the mountain trees;
Past the desert fly Huns' wild geese.
For thousands of miles, it's all blue;
While looking far away, I rue.

* New Peace: a former name for present-day Pin County in Sha'anhsi Province, which belonged to Ch'in in ancient times.
* Ch'in: the State of Ch'in (905 B.C.- 206 B.C.), one of the most powerful vassal states in the Chough dynasty, which developed into the first unified regime of China, i.e. the Ch'in Empire (221 B.C.- 206 B.C.).
* Hun: nomadic people north and west of China, often known as invaders, who had no trade but battle and carnage, no fields or plough lands but only wastes where white

bones lay scattered over yellow sands.
* wild goose: an undomesticated goose that is caring and responsible, taken as a symbol of benevolence, righteousness, good manner, wisdom, and faith in Chinese culture.

谒 老 君 庙

先君怀圣德，
灵庙肃神心。
草合人踪断，
尘浓鸟迹深。
流沙丹灶灭，
关路紫烟沉。
独伤千载后，
空馀松柏林。

A Visit to Laocius's Fane

To worship Laocius true and kind,
I come to the fane, clean my mind.
No footprints, grass and trailers creep,
With birds' track buried in dust deep.
You're gone, the incense burner out,
The pass so vague, are you about?
One thousand years now, I'm in pain;
The pines and cedars stand in vain;

* Laocius: Laocius (571 B.C.- 471 B.C.), born miraculously from the left side of the mother in the State of Ch'en (1046 B.C.- 478 B.C.) in the Shang dynasty (cir. 1600 B.C.-cir.1046 B.C.) as one source says. Surnamed Li, styled Ear and dubbed Bigshine, he was an under column historian, then an archive historian in the Chough House (1046 B.C.-256 B.C.), a position he served for more than eighty years (more than two hundred years according to *Historical Records*). He was the founder or one of the most influential philosophers of Wordism, the author of one of the most important

books in the world, that is, *The Word and the World*. Laocius's ideas, quietism in particular, have had a great influence on the development of Chinese philosophy as well as social and political development.

秋日登扬州西灵塔

宝塔凌苍苍，
登攀览四荒。
顶高元气合，
标出海云长。
万象分空界，
三天接画梁。
水摇金刹影，
日动火珠光。
鸟拂琼帘度，
霞连绣栱张。
目随征路断，
心逐去帆扬。
露浴梧楸白，
霜催橘柚黄。
玉毫如可见，
于此照迷方。

Climbing West Soul Pagoda in Yangchow on an Autumn Day

The pagoda o'errides the blue;
I climb up, every scene I view.
The top with vital air combine;
The spire presents a holy sign.
The things up or down one descries;
The painted beams hang in Three Skies.

The lake sways the shade of the fane;
The sun moves like a shining mane.
The warblers fly to the pearled screen;
The carved arch tilts to the cloud sheen.
My eyes follow the winding trail;
My heart chases the waving sail.
Dew glistens phoenix tree leaves dried;
Frost hastens oranges hue-dyed.
If the jade white hair can be found,
It'll light up the world all around.

* Yangchow: a city in today's Chiangsu Province and an important port city in the T'ang dynasty.
* Three Skies: a Buddhist term referring to the three realms in Buddhism.
* screen: a curtain which separates or cuts off, shelters or protects as a light partition, a common image in Chinese literature. A poem in *The Book of Songs* reads like this: "You wait for me before the screen; / Your hat-rings white do tinkle clean, / And your rubies brilliantly sheen."
* orange: a reddish, yellow, round, edible citrus fruit, with a sweet, juicy pulp; any of various evergreen trees (genus *Citrus*) of the rue family bearing this fruit.

登金陵冶城西北谢安墩

晋室昔横溃，
永嘉遂南奔。
沙尘何茫茫，
龙虎斗朝昏。
胡马风汉草，
天骄蹙中原。
哲匠感颓运，
云鹏忽飞翻。
组练照楚国，
旌旗连海门。
西秦百万众，
戈甲如云屯。
投鞭可填江，
一扫不足论。
皇运有返正，
丑虏无遗魂。
谈笑遏横流，
苍生望斯存。
冶城访古迹，
犹有谢安墩。
凭览周地险，
高标绝人喧。
想像东山姿，
缅怀右军言。
梧桐识嘉树，
蕙草留芳根。
白鹭映春洲，

青龙见朝暾。
地古云物在,
台倾禾黍繁。
我来酌清波,
于此树名园。
功成拂衣去,
归入武陵源。

Climbing Hsieh's Mound Northwest of Forgeton in Gold Hill

When there collapsed the House of Chin,
The people fled south, what a din!
Soil or dirt, sand or dust was whirled;
Ghosts and demons vied for the world.
The Hun horses galloped amain;
Chien Fu's troops did threaten Mid-plain.
The wise general did feel the trend;
He rose up to the land defend.
The armors shone on soldiers brave;
All flags, on banks and shore did wave.
Troops of West Ch'in a million strong,
Halberds, shields like clouds, what a throng.
The whips thrown could the river fill;
Chien Fu did boast he could all kill.
The royals came back to Right Way;
The clowns, routed, fled in dismay.
Between laughs, the currents Hsieh checked;
All people would pay their respect.
Now I come to the battleground

And here I can still find Hsieh's Mound.
Around, I o'erlook the terrain;
No more noise or din on the plain.
I now recall General Hsieh's poise
And think of Wang's persuading voice.
The phoenix tree loves the beau pine;
The orchid keeps its fragrance fine.
The egrets fly o'er the vernal stream;
The dragon greets the dawning beam.
Though old, the relics still remain;
Collapsed, the mound is lush with grain.
I'll drink a cup here in the breeze
And on the mound plant many trees.
When I succeed, I'd go afar
For free life there in Shangrila.

* Hsieh: referring to An Hsieh (A.D. 320 – A.D. 385), a general, statesman and renowned scholar in the Eastern Chin dynasty. He once lived in seclusion and went back to defend the country when Chien Fu sent troops to conquer Eastern Chin.
* Forgeton: a place for blacksmithing in the Three Kingdoms period located in Gold Hill, an alias of Gold Hill.
* Gold Hill: referring to Nanking, one of the most well-known ancient capitals in China.
* the House of Chin: In the Western Chin dynasty, there burst the most severe strife in the royal house which lasted sixteen years and involved more than eight lords.
* Chien Fu: Chien Fu (A.D. 338 – A.D. 385), a Lord of Fore-Ch'in in the Sixteen States period. During his reign, the state was booming in economy and military forces. Chien Fu wiped out several states in the north and unified the northern lands, but was defeated by An Hsieh, a commander of Eastern Chin, when Chien Fu sent his troops to the south.
* West Ch'in: indicating Fore-Ch'in (A.D. 350 – A.D. 394), one of the sixteen regimes in the Eastern Chin period.
* Wang: referring to Hsichih Wang (A.D. 303 – A.D. 379), a highborn calligrapher in the Eastern Chin dynasty, regarded as the Sage of Handwriting. He was a friend of An Hsieh's.

* orchid: a widely distributed family of terrestrial or epiphytic monocotyledonous plants, one of the four most important floral images in Chinese literature, which are wintersweet, orchid, bamboo and chrysanthemum.
* egret: a heron characterized, in the breeding season, by long and loose plumes drooping over the tail, usually white plumage.
* dragon: a fabulous serpent-like giant winged animal, a symbol of benevolence and sovereignty in Chinese culture.
* Shangrila: an ideal land free of tyranny and exploitation.

登瓦官阁

晨登瓦官阁，
极眺金陵城。
钟山对北户，
淮水入南荣。
漫漫雨花落，
嘈嘈天乐鸣。
两廊振法鼓，
四角吟风筝。
杳出霄汉上，
仰攀日月行。
山空霸气灭，
地古寒阴生。
寥廓云海晚，
苍茫宫观平。
门馀阊阖字，
楼识凤凰名。
雷作百山动，
神扶万栱倾。
灵光何足贵，
长此镇吴京。

Climbing to the Attic of Potter Temple

I climb Potter Temple at dawn
And overlook Gold Hill, the town.
North facing, there stands high Mt. Bell;

South running, the Huai seems to swell.
A murmur does sound like flowers rain;
The music rings sky-bound: fain, fain!
The corridor quakes with the drum;
The eaves sing to the wind: hum, hum.
The attic seems to reach the sky,
And touch the moon and sun on high.
The hills void, the royal vein dries;
The land old, how many woes rise?
At night the sea rolls without bound;
The temple looms as if there drowned.
"Heaven's Gate" is seen on the door;
The plague reads: Phoenixes to soar.
The thunders cause all hills to quake;
The deities prop arches that shake.
The Spirit Hall is such a crown
That safeguards Capital, our town.

* Potter Temple: a Buddhist temple located in today's Nanking, built in A.D. 364 during the Eastern Chin dynasty. It belongs in the Five Mountains and Ten Temples in China. It was so named because it was built on the site of the former Pottery Authorities, and after several reconstructions and renovations, it became a splendid large temple boasting one thousand monks in South China at the end of the Eastern Chin dynasty.
* Gold Hill: referring to Nanking, named after the Gold Hills nearby, one of the most well-known ancient cities in China, a strategic fort as a gateway to the sea, which has been the capital of Wu, Chin, and many other states or kingdoms, such as the six empires called Six Dynasties and has flourished immensely with increasing trade and travel.
* Mt. Bell: also known as Mt. Rosegold, located in the east of Gold Hill.
* the Huai: referring to the Ch'in Huai River flowing through Gold Hill, a cultural attraction.
* the Spirit Hall: an ancient palace.
* Capital: referring to Gold Hill, the former capitals of the Southern and Northern Dynasties.

登梅冈望金陵，赠族侄高座寺僧中孚

钟山抱金陵，
霸气昔腾发。
天开帝王居，
海色照宫阙。
群峰如逐鹿，
奔走相驰突。
江水九道来，
云端遥明没。
时迁大运去，
龙虎势休歇。
我来属天清，
登览穷楚越。
吾宗道门秀，
特异鸾凤骨。
众星罗青天，
明者独有月。
冥居顺生理，
草木不剪伐。
烟窗引蔷薇，
石壁老野蕨。
吴风谢安屐，
白足傲履袜。
几宿一下山，
萧然忘干谒。
谈经演金偈，
降鹤舞海雪。
时闻天香来，

了与世事绝。
佳游不可得,
春风惜远别。
赋诗留岩屏,
千载庶不灭。

Climbing Wintersweet Mound to Overlook Gold Hill and Dedicating a Verse to My Nephew, a Monk in High Seat Temple

Gold Hill is embraced by Mt. Bell;
The royal vein here used to swell.
The Lord's abode the sky does show;
To the palace the sea does glow.
The peaks look like stags and deer chased,
A-running side by side in haste.
From nine ways the river flows on;
Far off amid clouds it seems gone.
Time caused the royals to decline,
The dragons and tigers supine.
I come here for the broad clear skies,
With Ch'u and Yüeh before my eyes.
Out of the Li's you are the crest,
A phoenix spruce and a crane best.
The constellation in the sky,
Admired is the moon bright on high.
We'd withdraw and follow the Way;
No plants or grass will soon decay.
Mist thru the window wets the rose;
On the stone wall old wild fern grows.

In General Hsieh's shoes you are raised;

　　In White Feet socks you've bearings chaste.

　　A few nights here make my good stay;

　　I've forgotten all, rank or pay.

　　I discuss Gold Scriptures with you,

　　Like cranes dance over the white snow.

　　Sometimes I smell Heavenly balm,

　　Free from the dust, so free, so calm.

　　Best sights are beyond me and you;

　　The spring wind hates to say adieu.

　　I'll write a verse on the rock fast;

　　For thousands of years, it will last.

* Wintersweet Mound: 4.5 kilometers from Rivercalm, i.e., Gold Hill or present-day Nanking.
* High Seat Temple: a temple on Wintersweet Mound, also known as Sweet Dew Temple.
* Gold Hill: referring to Nanking, one of the most well-known ancient capitals in China.
* Mt. Bell: a mountain in Gold Hill, also known as Mt. Rosegold.
* Ch'u and Yüeh: two vassal states of Chough, referring to southeast part of China.
* phoenix: In Chinese mythology, the most beautiful bird, phoenix, only perches on phoenix trees, i.e. firmiana, only eats firmiana fruit, and only drinks sweet spring water, and this mythic bird appears only in times of peace and sagacious rule.
* crane: one of a family of large, long-necked, long-legged, heronlike birds allied to the rails, a symbol of integrity and longevity in Chinese culture, only second to the phoenix in cultural importance.
* rose: any of a genus of shrubs of the rose family, characteristically with prickly stems, alternate compound leaves, and five-parted, usually fragrant flowers of red, pink, white, yellow, etc, having many stamens. It is often used as a metaphor for beauty or love.
* General Hsieh: referring to An Hsieh (A.D. 320 - A.D. 385), a general, statesman and renowned scholar in the Eastern Chin dynasty. When Hsieh was playing chess with his friends, a letter arrived but Hsieh continued to play chess without a single hint after reading it. His guest asked him about the letter, he answered in calmness:"My son has

defeated the enemy." Not until Hsieh went back to his room did he realize that he was too happy to find his shoes had already broken.

* White Feet: a monk of high reputation in the Chin dynasty.
* Gold Scriptures: referring to Buddhist classics, such as *Veda*, *The Diamond Sutra*, *Prajna Paramita* and so on.

登金陵凤凰台

凤凰台上凤凰游，
凤去台空江自流。
吴宫花草埋幽径，
晋代衣冠成古丘。
三山半落青天外，
二水中分白鹭洲。
总为浮云能蔽日，
长安不见使人愁。

Climbing Phoenix Mound in Gold Hill

On Phoenix Mound phoenixes used to play;
Phoenixes gone, mound bare, River flows sole.
The blooms in Wu's Palace fall to the clay;
The crown of Chin's power has become a knoll.
Three mounts stretch, half on earth, half to the sky;
Both banks see waters by Egret Shoal run.
To Long Peace beyond me I can but sigh.
For hanging clouds there will eclipse the sun.

* phoenix: an auspicious bird, the best of all, which only perches on parasol trees and eats bamboo shoots and pearly stone according to legend.
* Gold Hill: referring to Nanking, one of the most well-known ancient capitals in China.
* Wu's Palace: In the Three Kingdoms period, the Kingdom of Wu established its capital in Gold Hill.
* Chin: referring to the Eastern Chin whose capital was Gold Hill.

* Egret Shoal: an ancient shoal in the middle of the Yangtze River.
* Long Peace: referring to Ch'ang'an if transliterated, the metropolis of gold, the capital of the T'ang Empire, present-day Hsi-an, the capital of Sha'anhsi Province.

望庐山瀑布

Gazing at the Mt. Lodge Waterfall

其 一

西登香炉峰,
南见瀑布水。
挂流三百丈,
喷壑数十里。
欻如飞电来,
隐若白虹起。
初惊河汉落,
半洒云天里。
仰观势转雄,
壮哉造化功。
海风吹不断,
江月照还空。
空中乱潈射,
左右洗青壁;
飞珠散轻霞,
流沫沸穹石。
而我乐名山,
对之心益闲;
无论漱琼液,
还得洗尘颜。
且谐宿所好,
永愿辞人间。

No.1

I climb up the Censer from west,
And from north you see water fall.
The fall roars miles down without rest;
Its gush is dozens of miles in all.
It pours like a lightning ray;
It looms like a white rainbow rise.
It drops like the bright Milky Way;
It splashes off, half down the skies.
Looking up, you see its airs proud,
By nature made, by it enjoyed.
Sea wind can't blow it off tho loud;
The river moon returns to the void.
It spurts about high in the air;
Left and right the crag it washes.
The drops fly onto clouds so fair;
Up and down the rock it crashes.
All mountains please me as they do;
Before the fall, I feel inspired.
We can drink nectar, it is true,
Or wash our face to be retired.
With my old friends I will here stay;
For aye from dust I keep away.

* Mt. Lodge: a famous mountain with historic, cultural and religious attractions, an especially sacred place to Wordists, about 5,000 feet high, in present-day Chianghsi Province.
* the Censer: a scenic peak of Mt. Lodge, looking like an incense burner.
* the bright Milky Way: the Silver River in Chinese mythology, the Milky Way, a luminous band circling the heavens composed of stars and nebulae; the Galaxy.

* nectar: in Chinese and Greek mythologies, the drink of the gods or fairies, and in botany, the saccharine substance secreted by some plants and forming the base of natural honey.

其 二

日照香炉生紫烟，
遥看瀑布挂前川。
飞流直下三千尺，
疑是银河落九天。

No. 2

Purple smoke o'er the Censer in sun-light,
The waterfall afar hangs like cloth white.
A thousand fathoms down the river flies,
Like the Milky Way falling from the skies.

* the Censer: a scenic peak of Mt. Lodge, looking like an incense burner, especially when mist hangs over it.
* the Milky Way: a luminous band circling the heavens composed of stars and nebulae, also known as the Galaxy.

登庐山五老峰

庐山东南五老峰，
青天削出金芙蓉。
九江秀色可揽结，
吾将此地巢云松。

Climbing the Five Old Men Peaks on Mt. Lodge

South of Mt. Lodge are the Five Old Men Peaks,
Like golden lilies with colored clouds dressed.
The charm of Nine Rivers everyone seeks;
In this place I would with clouds and pines rest.

* the Five Old Men Peaks: referring to five adjacent peaks standing like five old men.
* Mt. Lodge: a famous mountain with historic, cultural and religious attractions, located in present-day Chianghsi Province.
* Nine Rivers: referring to Bankshine, a river town, which is present-day Chiuchiang, Chianghsi Province, where Mt. Lodge is located.

江上望皖公山

奇峰出奇云，
秀木含秀气。
清晏皖公山，
嶷绝称人意。
独游沧江上，
终日淡无味。
但爱兹岭高，
何由讨灵异。
默然遥相许，
欲往心莫遂。
待吾还丹成，
投迹归此地。

Looking at Mt. Wan from the River

Bizarre clouds do bizarre peaks greet；
Graceful air does graceful woods meet；
Mt. Lord Wan looks calm and at ease；
The steep crags my spirits do please.
Alone I cruise the River blue，
All's tasteless and I'm listless，too.
But I love this mountain so high；
How could I into magics pry?
O Lord Wan, promise you I may，
As it's not time for me to stay.
I'll come to this place where you are

With elixir from cinnabar.

* Mt. Wan: also known as Mt. Lord Wan, a mountain in Anhui Province, which was Lord Wan's feoff in ancient times.
* the River: the Yangtze River.
* Lord Wan: a count whose feoff was in Mt. Lurking (Mt. Chien if transliterated) in the Chough dynasty. He was stationed there as a monitor of the State of Hsu.
* With elixir from cinnabar: Wordists seeking immortality, besides looking for death-conquering herbs, have gone all out to make pellets with such materials as refined cinnabar.

望 黄 鹤 山

东望黄鹤山，
雄雄半空出。
四面生白云，
中峰倚红日。
岩峦行穹跨，
峰嶂亦冥密。
颇闻列仙人，
于此学飞术。
一朝向蓬海，
千载空石室。
金灶生烟埃，
玉潭秘清谧。
地古遗草木，
庭寒老芝术。
蹇予羡攀跻，
因欲保闲逸。
观奇遍诸岳，
兹岭不可匹。
结心寄青松，
永悟客情毕。

Staring at Mt. Yellow Crane

At Mt. Yellow Crane east I stare;
Its power does domineer the air.
From all around white clouds arise;

The mid peak on the sun relies.
The ranges hang high in suspense;
The peaks rise out of mist so dense.
Lots of immortals, I oft hear,
Come to learn the art of flight here.
Once they fly to the Isles in brume,
Void for ages will be Stone Room.
The metal stove lies waste like this,
With ripples tired on the abyss.
The old ground is lush with cold weeds;
The cold yard sees old herbal seeds.
This mountain I'd climb and climb higher
To quench my free-going desire.
I've sought wondrous peaks everywhere,
But no one can with this compare.
To pines I'll give my heart to rest;
Enlightened, I shan't be a guest.

* Mt. Yellow Crane: a mountain in today's Wuhan, Hupei Province.
* the Isles: an ideal imaginary place consisting of three isles in East Sea, where fairies and immortals live.
* Stone Room: unidentified.
* the metal stove: the stove wherewith alchemists smelt cinnabar or other materials for elixirs.

鹦鹉洲

鹦鹉来过吴江水,
江上洲传鹦鹉名。
鹦鹉西飞陇山去,
芳洲之树何青青。
烟开兰叶香风暖,
岸夹桃花锦浪生。
迁客此时徒极目,
长洲孤月向谁明。

Parrot Shoal

The parrot's come to the Wu, as is heard;
The river or the shoal all know the bird.
The parrot has flown west to the Bulge Hills;
The grass on the shoal a balmy song trills.
The balm of orchids does the mist pervade;
Peach blossoms on the banks roll like brocade.
I, exiled, gaze in vain beyond my sight;
To whom does Luna o'er the shoal shine bright?

* Parrot Shoal: a shoal located in Wuhan, Hupei Province. It is named after *Ode to the Parrot* by Scale Mi (A.D. 173 - A.D. 198), a brilliant and arrogant man in the Three Kingdoms period. When Heng was banished to Wuhan, the magistrate gave him a parrot and required him to write a verse about it. Heng wrote *Ode to the Parrot*, more than 600 words at a breath, comparing the parrot to himself.
* the Wu: the river outside of Mightboom, one of the three towns that make today's Wuhan.

* the Bulge Hills: also called Mt. Bulge, south of today's Ninghsia and west of today's Sha'anhsi, a borderline between Sha'anhsi Loess Plateau and West Bulge Loess Plateau.
* orchid: a terrestrial or epiphytic monocotyledonous plant having thickened bulbous roots and often very showy distinctive flowers, one of the four most important floral images in Chinese literature, which are wintersweet, orchid, bamboo and chrysanthemum.

九日登巴陵置酒望洞庭水军

九日天气清，
登高无秋云。
造化辟川岳，
了然楚汉分。
长风鼓横波，
合沓蹙龙文。
忆昔传游豫，
楼船壮横汾。
今兹讨鲸鲵，
旌旆何缤纷。
白羽落酒樽，
洞庭罗三军。
黄花不掇手，
战鼓遥相闻。
剑舞转颓阳，
当时日停曛。
酣歌激壮士，
可以摧妖氛。
握觯东篱下，
渊明不足群。

Looking at the Fleet on Lake Cavehall While Drinking at the Pa Hills

Double Ninth Day is a bright day;
No clouds on high, no clouds astray.

Nature's made all, river and mound;
Between Ch'u and Han lies a bound.
The high wind on the river raves,
To form surging dragon-like waves.
As is said, Lord Martial came then;
His tower ships filled the River Fen.
The warship will wipe out the whales;
Here flow the flags, there wave the sails.
The army on Cavehall line up;
The white plumed arrows shade their cup.
No time for chrysanthemums sweet,
The war drums loudly they fast beat.
The sword play boosts the setting sun;
That gives off shining light anon.
The song of wine sends them a joy
So that they can demons destroy.
Now we keep away from East Fence;
I shan't drink with the hermit hence.

* Lake Cavehall: a large lake in today's Hunan Province.
* the Pa Hills: referring to Hillshine, located in present-day Yüehyang, Hunan Province.
* Double Ninth Day: a festival on the ninth day of the ninth month in Chinese Lunar calendar. There is a long tradition that people go climbing and enjoy chrysanthemums on this day.
* Between Ch'u and Han lies a bound: referring to the war between Hsiang Yü's Ch'u army and Pang Liu's Han army. In the summer of 205 B.C., Yü Hsiang defeated the Han troops, which retreated to Hsingshine on the south bank of the Yellow River. The war lasted for two years.
* Lord Martial: Emperor Martial (156 B.C.- 87 B.C.), the seventh emperor of Han, a prominent statesman, strategist and poet, and a pursuer of immortality as well.
* His tower ships filled the River Fen: Emperor Martial had a symposium with his ministers on the tower ship in the River Fen, the second largest branch of the Yellow River and here composed his *Ode to Autumn Wind*: On the River Fen my tower ship

does cruise, / While ploughing the blue and splashing the waves.
* whale: a cetaceous mammal of fish-like form, especially one of the larger pelagic species, as distinguished from dolphins and porpoises, reffering to Lushan An's rebels.
* chrysanthemum: any of a genus of perennials (*Chrysanthemum*) of the composite family, some cultivated varieties of which have large heads of showy flowers of various colors, a symbol of purity or longevity in Chinese culture.
* East Fence: an allusion to Poolbright T'ao's retiring life when the poet gathered chrysanthemums under East Fence and looked at the southern hills at leisure.

秋登巴陵望洞庭

清晨登巴陵,
周览无不极。
明湖映天光,
彻底见秋色。
秋色何苍然,
际海俱澄鲜。
山青灭远树,
水绿无寒烟。
来帆出江中,
去鸟向日边。
风清长沙浦,
山空云梦田。
瞻光惜颓发,
阅水悲徂年。
北渚既荡漾,
东流自潺湲。
郢人唱白雪,
越女歌采莲。
听此更肠断,
凭崖泪如泉。

Gazing at Cavehall on the Pa's Mound on an Autumn Day

At dawn I climb up the Pa's mound
And I can see all scenes around.

Lake Cavehall mirrors the sun light;
The lake bed shows the autumn bright.
The autumn shows much blue or green;
The shore and water are both clean,
The green hills dim the far-off trees;
The blue waves stir up no cold breeze.
The boats downstream so lightly run;
The birds are in flight to the sun.
The wind sweeps Long Sand and its shore;
Frost has all thawed on Cloud Dream Moor.
The autumn has made my hair gray;
The water sends my prime away.
The north shoal fluctuates with ripples;
The east flow shimmers with gurgles.
The Ying man sings the song *White Snow*;
The Yüeh girl hums *Pick Lotus, Go*.
These songs do make a vagrant sad;
Beside the cliff, tears drip like mad.

* Cavehall: Lake Cavehall, a large lake in today's Hunan Province.
* The Pa's Mound: referring to Hillshine, present-day Yüehyang, Hunan Province.
* Long Sand: Ch'angsha if transliterated, the capital city of present-day Hunan Province.
* Cloud Dream Moor: a general name for the lakes on Chianghan Plain, Hupei.
* Ying: the capital of the State of Ch'u in the Eastern Chough dynasty, and an alternative name for the lands in present-day Hupei and northern Hunan.
* White Snow: an elegant song in the ancient times.
* Yüeh: the State of Yüeh (2032 B.C.- 222 B.C.), a vassal state under Chough in Southeast China in the Spring and Autumn period. As a regime it preceded Chough, first founded by Nothing Left (Wuyü), King Young Health (Shaok'ang) of Hsia' son born of a concubine.
* *Pick Lotus, Go*: an ancient song. When gathering lotus seeds, gatherers usually sing this song.

与夏十二登岳阳楼

楼观岳阳尽,
川迥洞庭开。
雁引愁心去,
山衔好月来。
云间连下榻,
天上接行杯。
醉后凉风起,
吹人舞袖回。

On the Hillshine Tower with Hsia Twelve

On Hillshine Tower I look around;
The river flows, for Cavehall bound.
The wild geese take away my woe;
The hill holds up a disc of glow.
The table's set upstairs, so high,
Like we'll have our feast in the sky.
While we are drunk there blows a sough;
Our sleeves blown up, we go home now.

* the Hillshine Tower: a tower with tourist attractions located in present-day Hillshine (Yüehyang), Hunan Province.
* Cavehall: Lake Cavehall, one of the largest lakes in China and many cultural attractions.
* wild goose: an undomesticated goose that is caring and responsible, taken as a symbol of benevolence, righteousness, good manner, wisdom and faith in Chinese culture.

登巴陵开元寺西阁赠衡岳僧方外

衡岳有开士,
五峰秀真骨。
见君万里心,
海水照秋月。
大臣南溟去,
问道皆请谒。
洒以甘露言,
清凉润肌发。
明湖落天镜,
香阁凌银阙。
登眺餐惠风,
新花期启发。

Dedication to Monk Outworld in West Hall of Allbegun Temple on the Pa's Mound

On Mt. Scale, Buddha smiles alone;
The Five Peaks show the real head bone.
I see you'll tour the world afar;
The sea reflects the autumn star.
Great monk, to South Sea you'll depart;
When asking way, you show your heart.
You speak out words like pearls of dew,
Which moistens hair and skin with hue.
To Lake Bright, Sky Mirror does fall,
Which lights up Aromatic Hall.

Upstairs on spring breeze we will dine;
The new blooms will give a new sign.

* Allbegun Temple: in either of the two capitals and every prefecture of T'ang, there was a temple called Great Cloud Temple and changed to Allbegun Temple in the Allbegun reign of the T'ang Empire.
* the Pa's Mound: referring to Hillshine, present-day Yüehyang, Hunan Province.
* Mt. Scale: one of the Five Mountains in China, located in Hunan Province, along with Mt. Ever in Shanhsi, Mt. Arch in Shantung, Mt. Flora in Sha'anhsi, and Mt. Tower in Honan.
* Buddha: the Enlightened in a literal sense; an incarnation of selflessness, virtue and wisdom; specifically, Gautama Siddhartha (cir. 563 B.C.- cir. 483 B.C.), the founder of Buddhism, regarded by his followers as the last of a series of deified religious teachers of central and eastern Asia.
* the Five Peaks: As legend goes, a monk met an immortal, and the next day he had a bad headache. As he was about to cure, there was a voice coming from above, telling him his head bone was changing. Then, his head bone swelled as if five peaks soared.
* South Sea: today's South China Sea, in the south of China.
* Lake Bright: a lake that is like a bright mirror from the sky.
* Sky Mirror: a metaphor for the lake mentioned in the poem.
* Aromatic Hall: According to *The Vimalakirti Sutra*, in a remote domain in the cosmos there is a kingdom called Aroma and in Aroma there lives a Buddha called Aromatic. And in the kingdom all buildings are made of aromatic stuff.

与贾至舍人于龙兴寺剪落梧桐枝望灉湖

剪落青梧枝，
灉湖坐可窥。
雨洗秋山净，
林光澹碧滋。
水闲明镜转，
云绕画屏移。
千古风流事，
名贤共此时。

Looking at Lake Rush with Chih Chia, Scribe of Privy Council, at Dragonrise Temple, Holding a Phoenix Tree Spray

I cut a spray off Phoenix Tree;
So sitting, Lake Rush I can see.
The rain has washed the hills so clean;
The trees give off an oily sheen.
The water like glass turns around,
As if the screen did move aground.
To gather with you, the great sages,
Is our great hour to chew for ages.

* Lake Rush: also known as Lake Backflow which is south of Hillshine. As it is dry in winter and spring, it is also called Lake Dry.
* Dragonrise Temple: no longer existing in the T'ang dynasty, with only relics east of Great Peace Temple.

* Phoenix Tree: Chinese parasol tree, so named because phoenixes perch on Chinese parasol trees.
* screen: a curtain which separates or cuts off, shelters or protects as a light partition, a common image in Chinese literature. Two lines from a Sung lyric by Haowen Yüan reads like this:"The drizzle falls before my tower's sill; / 'Broidered with crabapples, the screen's chill."

挂席江上待月有怀

待月月未出，
望江江自流。
倏忽城西郭，
青天悬玉钩。
素华虽可揽，
清景不同游。
耿耿金波里，
空瞻鸦鹊楼。

Setting Sail and Waiting for Luna

I wait for Luna; it does not show!
I look at the River; it'd fain flow!
West of the town we soon come by,
A disc of moon hung in the sky.
Although the glow you can well touch,
I don't like the play very much.
Amid waves of moonbeams so gilt,
I only see Magpie Tower tilt.

* Luna: the moon, an important image in Chinese literature, symbolizing solitude or happy reunions.
* the River: referring to the Long River, the longest river in China and one of the longest in the world.
* Magpie Tower: a building in Gold Hills.

金陵望汉江

汉江回万里，
派作九龙盘。
横溃豁中国，
崔嵬飞迅湍。
六帝沦亡后，
三吴不足观。
我君混区宇，
垂拱众流安。
今日任公子，
沧浪罢钓竿。

Gazing at the Han River from Gold Hill

The Han flows three thousand miles long,
Nine branches like dragons there flung.
The overflow floods the land vast;
The torrents surge up and sweep fast.
The Six Dynasties' pride decays;
The Three Wus are not worth a praise.
Our Lord rules the universe great;
Inaction leads to a good state.
If Prince of Jen came here today,
He'd throw his fish hook to the bay.

* the Han River: the longest branch of the Long River, which has an important position in Chinese history.

* Gold Hill: referring to Nanking, one of the most well-known ancient capitals in China.
* dragon: Though variously understood as a large reptile, a marine monster, a jackal and so on in Western culture, it has been esteemed as a fabulous serpent-like giant winged animal, a totem of the Chinese nation and a symbol of benevolence and sovereignty in Chinese culture.
* the Six Dynasties: the six different regimes of Wu, Chin, Sung, Ch'i, Liang, and Ch'en that had Gold Hill as their capital are regarded as six dynasties in Chinese history.
* the Three Wus: Wu was divided into three parts, Wu Rise, Wu County and Summit in the Han dynasty.
* Prince of Jen: a legendary figure recorded in *Sir Lush*. Prince Jen was good at fishing. He fished at East Sea with a huge hook and fifty bulls. Having been waiting on Mt. Summit for a year, he did not get any. Not long after, he caught a fish big enough to feed the people from Chechiang to Mt. Green Tree. Prince Jen, lofty and broadminded, has been regarded as a supramundane figure in Chinese literature.

秋登宣城谢朓北楼

江城如画里，
山晓望晴空。
两水夹明镜，
双桥落彩虹。
人烟寒橘柚，
秋色老梧桐。
谁念北楼上，
临风怀谢公。

An Autumn Afternoon on the North Tower Built by T'iao Hsieh in Hsuan

The river town's like a picture;
The hills watch the sky in sunglow.
Both rivers hold out a mirror;
Either bridge is a dropped rainbow.
The smoke chills the tangerine grove;
The fall ages the phoenix trees.
The tower sees my nostalgia rove;
Who knows I miss Hsieh in the breeze?

* T'iao Hsieh: T'iao Hsieh (A.D. 464 – A.D. 499), Hue by courtesy name, an outstanding highborn landscape poet. He was appointed prefecture of Hsuan in A.D. 495 and then director of the Board of Civil Affairs, and died in prison due to a false charge.

* Hsuan: an ancient town in today's Anhui Province, a county instituted in the early years of the Ch'in Emperor under the Prefecture of Redshine. It became a prefecture in 281 during the Chin dynasty. It is well known for rich historical legacies, and best remembered for its high-quality rice paper.
* tangerine: a variety of Mandarin orange with a deep-reddish-yellow color and segments that are easily separated.

望 天 门 山

天门中断楚江开，
碧水东流直北回。
两岸青山相对出，
孤帆一片日边来。

Watching Mt. Skygate

The Ch'u River cuts Mt. Skygate in twain
And flows east, then north, not bending again.
On the banks green peaks face to face appear;
A lonely sail against the sun comes near.

* Mt. Skygate: mountains located on the banks of the Yangtze River, one mountain on the northern bank, and the other on the southern. The two mountains stand opposite like a gate of the river, hence the name.
* the Ch'u River: referring to the Long River because it flows on what was Ch'u's land.

望木瓜山

早起见日出，
暮见栖鸟还。
客心自酸楚，
况对木瓜山。

Gazing at Mt. Pawpaw

My morning rise sees the sun rise;
The evening sees birds back home fly.
I ask the alien land painful whys,
And stand before Mt. Pawpaw high.

* Mt. Pawpaw: There are many mountains bearing this name in China. This mountain may be the one in Constant Virtue (Ch'angte) or the one in Poolton (Ch'ihchow). Pai Li was once in Constant Virtue on his way to exile in Nightboy and he once toured to Poolton.

登敬亭北二小山，余时送客，逢崔侍御，并登此地

送客谢亭北，
逢君纵酒还。
屈盘戏白马，
大笑上青山。
回鞭指长安，
西日落秦关。
帝乡三千里，
杳在碧云间。

Meeting Ts'ui, the Royal Servant, While Seeing Off My Guest and Climbing Two Small Hills North of Mt. Chingt'ing with Him

North Hsieh's Kiosk I see off my guest;
You come back from a feast to rest.
Your white horse enjoys your horse play;
Climbing uphill, you laugh your way.
You point your whip to Long Peace as
The sun's setting west of Ch'in Pass.
Capital's one thousand miles far,
As far off as the farthest star.

* Mt. Chingt'ing: a mountain with literary attractions, located nearby Hsuan, an offset of Mt. Yellow, consisting of 60 peaks, rolling more than three miles and 317 meters above sea level.

* Hsieh's Kiosk: located in Hsuan where T'iao Hsieh, a landscape poet, saw off his friend.
* Long Peace: Ch'ang'an if transliterated, the capital of the T'ang Empire, present-day His'an, West Peace literally. It saw the wonder of the age that reached the pinnacle of brilliance in Emperor Deepsire's reign: The main castle with its nine-fold gates, the thirty-six imperial palaces, pillars of gold, innumerable mansions and villas of noblemen, the broad avenues thronged with motley crowds of townsmen and gallants on horseback, and mandarin cars drawn by yokes of black oxen, countless taverns and houses of pleasure, which opened their doors by night all made this city a kaleidoscope of miracles.
* Ch'in Pass: referring to Case Dale or the land west of Case Dale.

过崔八丈水亭

高阁横秀气，
清幽并在君。
檐飞宛溪水，
窗落敬亭云。
猿啸风中断，
渔歌月里闻。
闲随白鸥去，
沙上自为群。

Seeing Old Ts'ui Eight at Riverine Pavilion

The pavilion shows budding grace;
Looking out, you find a quiet place.
To the Wan stream the eaves will fly;
To the window fall clouds on high.
There in the wind the monkeys cry;
A moonlit fisher's song comes by.
We should fly with seagulls when free;
On the sand a flock we can be.

* the Wan Stream: located in the north of Gold Hill.
* seagull: a kind of sea bird, any gull or large tern, a symbol of clean integrity. The seagulls in the Wordist book *Sir Line* (Liehtzu) are particularly sensitive to impurity of motive and will make friends only with the completely guileless and disinterested.

登广武古战场怀古

秦鹿奔野草,
逐之若飞蓬。
项王气盖世,
紫电明双瞳。
呼吸八千人,
横行起江东。
赤精斩白帝,
叱咤入关中。
两龙不并跃,
五纬与天同。
楚灭无英图,
汉兴有成功。
按剑清八极,
归酣歌大风。
伊昔临广武,
连兵决雌雄。
分我一杯羹,
太皇乃汝翁。
战争有古迹,
壁垒颓层穹。
猛虎啸洞壑,
饥鹰鸣秋空。
翔云列晓阵,
杀气赫长虹。
拨乱属豪圣,
俗儒安可通。
沉湎呼竖子,

狂言非至公。
抚掌黄河曲，
嗤嗤阮嗣宗。

Reminiscing the Past in Broad Mars Battlefield

A deer chased in grass is the crown;
It's chased like flying thistledown.
Over the world Hsiang's power did rise;
Like lightening were his bright eyes.
Eight thousand men he did command,
And crossed the river to East Land.
Liu, when drunk, did White God wipe out
And entered Midland with a shout.
Now two dragons would deadly vie,
As was the course set by the sky.
To realize his great aim Hsiang failed;
To his own victory Liu hailed.
With his sword he settled the world
And sang his *High Wind* as if whirled.
Back in those years the two men fought;
Each would fight the other to naught.
"Cook my father, and give me stew;
My father is your father, too."
But relics of war, time elapsed;
Neath the sky the barracks collapsed.
In the deep cave fierce tigers howl;
In the broad sky hungry hawks growl.
The clouds float before the array;

Their shouts scare the rainbow to ray.
To settle the world needs saints true;
What can a studious scholar do?
When drunk, Juan cursed Liu as a cad;
That's unfair with all those words mad.
Lo, the Yellow River laughs out:
Juan, what are you talking about?

* Broad Mars Battlefield: an ancient battlefield where the Han and the Western Ch'u fought to win the new regime.
* deer: a ruminant (family *Cervidae*), having deciduous antlers, usually in the male only, as the moose, elk, and reindeer. Deer are closely related to Chinese life. Deer hide is a precious gift, especially presented to a female and a deer is usually a symbol of imperial power as it is often a target of pursuit.
* thistledown: the pappus of a thistle; the ripe silky fibers from the dry flower of a thistle, a metaphor for drifting or wandering.
* Hsiang: referring to Yü Hsiang (232 B.C.- 202 B.C.), Overlord of Western Ch'u, who was strong and had two pupils in each of his eyes as historical records tell us.
* Liu: referring to Pang Liu (256 B.C.- 195 B.C.), Lord Highsire of Han, the founding lord of Han. Pang Liu killed a snake on road, and later, an old woman mourned for the dead snake and said it was a son of White God.
* White God: the god in charge of the west, one of the five heavenly lords in Chinese mythology.
* *High Wind*: a song written by Pang Liu when he went back to his homeland, which reads like this: A high wind rises; o the clouds wave. / I overpower the world, o home I crave. / To guard my land, o where can I find the brave?
* Cook my father, and give me stew; / My father is your father, too: Pang Liu and Yü Hsiang were sworn brothers before. When Hsiang captured Liu's father and threatened Liu, Liu replied him with these words to recriminate.
* Juan: referring to Chi Juan (A.D. 210 - A.D. 263), a poet in the Chin dynasty, and Hsien Juan, a renowned scholar and the nephew of Chi, both of them were among the Seven Sages of Bamboo Groves. Chi once went to Broad Mars and scorned at Pang Liu.

古近体诗五十八首
Old-new Rhythmic Poetry, 58 Poems

安州应城玉女汤作

神女殁幽境,
汤池流大川。
阴阳结炎炭,
造化开灵泉。
地底烁朱火,
沙旁歊素烟。
沸珠跃明月,
皎镜涵空天。
气浮兰芳满,
色涨桃花然。
精览万殊入,
潜行七泽连。
愈疾功莫尚,
变盈道乃全。
濯缨掬清泚,
晞发弄潺湲。
散下楚王国,
分浇宋玉田。
可以奉巡幸,
奈何隔穷偏。
独随朝宗水,
赴海输微涓。

The Fairy Hotspring in Ying, Peaceton

The fairy died here, so calm, who

Became a spring and downstream flew.
So burning out of Shade and Shine,
Appeared there a hot spring divine.
A flame there must be underground;
The sand knoll sees white brume around.
The pool looks like Luna it seems,
Or a mirror that's filled with gleams.
The orchid fragrance lures your nose;
Your face shines like a peach that blows.
It holds essence from all around
And links lakes and moors underground.
A cure it is without compare;
It's made to wax, wean, gloom or glare.
It's clear while hot gas floats on high;
Your hair immersed is soon to dry.
The old Ch'u State it permeates;
Yü Sung's farmland it irrigates.
His Majesty could take a bath;
It's too far—there's not e'en a path.
It joins the mainstream to the sea
To contribute a bit, a small wee.

* Ying: Yingshine or Yington under the Prefecture of Peaceton, in present-day Piety (Hsiaokan), Hupei Province.
* Peaceton: one of the 360 prefectures of the T'ang Empire in today's Hupei Province.
* Shade and Shine: the most important and basic concept of Chinese or Eastern philosophy, characterized by three features: identification, opposition and interconversion, although apparently standing for two poles of binary opposition.
* peach: any of the plant (*Prunus Percica*), bearing a fleshy, juicy, edible drupe, cultivated in many varieties in temperate zones considered sacred in China, often used as a metaphor for a young woman, as a section of a poem in *The Book of Songs* reads: "The peach twigs sway, / Ablaze the flower; / Now she's married away, / Befitting

her new bower."
* the old Ch'u State: one of the most powerful and largest vassal states of Chough.
* Jade Sung: Jade Sung (cir. 298 B.C.- cir. 222 B.C.), a student of Yüan Ch'ü's, and a verse writer in the Warring States period. He once served as an official for King Hsiang of Ch'u. When King Hsiang traveled to Clouds Moor, he promised his retinues a farmland in Clouds Moor if any of them could write a verse, and Sung won the land.

之广陵宿常二南郭幽居

绿水接柴门，
有如桃花源。
忘忧或假草，
满院罗丛萱。
暝色湖上来，
微雨飞南轩。
故人宿茅宇，
夕鸟栖杨园。
还惜诗酒别，
深为江海言。
明朝广陵道，
独忆此倾樽。

Putting Up for the Night in Ch'ang Two's Quiet Abode in Broadridge

The stream links with the wicker gate;
It's like a fairyland, so great.
Your yard's full of tiger lilies;
With the grass we kill our worries.
The lake beholds afterglow shine;
Your window greets a drizzle fine.
My friend, you live in this thatched shack
While birds to your poplars fly back.
I will cherish this verse and wine
And your words as deep as the brine.

I'm leaving Broadridge tomorrow;
Our cups are filled with our sorrow.

* Fairyland: an ideal abode for immortals, sometimes thought of as being in the middle of East Sea, sometimes in the sky.
* poplar: any of a genus (*Populus*) of dioecious trees and bushes of the willow family, widely distributed in the northern hemisphere.
* Broadbridge: an alternative name for Yangchow, an important city on the Peking-Hangchow Canal.

夜下征虏亭

船下广陵去，
月明征虏亭。
山花如绣颊，
江火似流萤。

Beat Foe Bower Under Night

To Broadridge my boat is to go
From the moonlit bower called Beat Foe.
Hill blossoms are like girls' cheeks bright;
Fireworm-like is the fishing light.

* Beat Foe Bower: an ancient kiosk in Gold Hill built by Shih Hsieh, a general in the Eastern Chin dynasty.
* Broadbridge: an alternative name for Yangchow, in present-day Chiangsu Province.
* fireworm: also called firefly or glowworm, which appears in or over grass at night and can be put in a transparent bottle or jade pot to offer light.

下途归石门旧居

吴山高，越水清，
握手无言伤别情。
将欲辞君挂帆去，
离魂不散烟郊树。
此心郁怅谁能论，
有愧叨承国士恩。
云物共倾三月酒，
岁时同饯五侯门。
羡君素书尝满案，
含丹照白霞色烂。
余尝学道穷冥筌，
梦中往往游仙山。
何当脱屣谢时去，
壶中别有日月天。
俯仰人间易凋朽，
钟峰五云在轩牖。
惜别愁窥玉女窗，
归来笑把洪崖手。
隐居寺，隐居山，
陶公炼液栖其间。
凝神闭气昔登攀，
恬然但觉心绪闲。
数人不知几甲子，
昨夜犹带冰霜颜。
我离虽则岁物改，
如今了然失所在。
别君莫道不尽欢，

悬知乐客遥相待。
石门流水遍桃花,
我亦曾到秦人家。
不知何处得鸡豕,
就中仍见繁桑麻。
翛然远与世事间,
装鸾驾鹤又复远。
何必长从七贵游,
劳生徒聚万金产。
挹君去,长相思,
云游雨散从此辞。
欲知怅别心易苦,
向暮春风杨柳丝。

Returning to the Old Abode at Stone Gate

Wu's mountains are high, and Yüeh's water blue;
Hand in hand, speechless, we can't check our rue.
Now I will go, and high set is my sail;
The parting soul o'er the trees does not fail.
The melancholy in my heart who knows?
I feel ashamed with your praise so profuse.
The third moon in the town we had our cheers,
And attended feasts in the halls of peers.
Books of the Word on your desk I admire;
Silk covers and red words gleamed like a fire.
I used to learn the Word and realms explore;
In my dreams I would o'er fairy hills soar.
I would take off my dusty shoes one day
And in the Pot with fairies I would stay.

Life, so short, like blossoms, is soon to end,
And like white clouds over Mt. Bell suspend.
When you left, I gazed to your screen, so sad;
When you came back I shook your hand, so glad.
The temple you face, and the hill you face;
Lord Glee practiced there and we find his trace.
I gazed, held my breath and climbed up the mound,
And suddenly felt raised, looking around.
A few didn't know how long they'd whiled,
With skin like snow, each smiling like a child.
Since I left there everything's changed each year;
I know what has happened to it, I'm quite clear.
Don't sigh at this feast that we've no more glee;
The poets and drinkers o'er there will feast me.
At Stone Gate peach blossoms with the stream flew;
I went to the Ch'in refugees there, too.
Where did they get the pig, chickens, all food?
Their homes were well girded by mulberry wood.
They freely lived, away from world affair;
Oft, they went astride cranes, I don't know where.
Why should I go with those peers and those lords;
They may have piled gold in vain in their hoards.
Now I go from you; endless is my woe;
No more it rains, and clouds go from the blue.
If you will know how hard it is to part,
Just look how the willow waves to my heart.

* Stone Gate: Mt. Stone Gate, a mountain 30 kilometers from today's Tangt'u Anhui Province, another mountain having the same name in present-day Ch'ingt'ien, Chechiang Province. Stone Gate in this poem is probably the latter.

* the Word: referring to Tao if transliterated, the most significant and profoundest

concept in Chinese philosophy. According to Laocius's *The Word and the World*: "The Word is void, but its use is infinite. O deep! It seems to be the root of all things."
* Pot: There was an immortal who had a pot, in which a whole world hid.
* Mt. Bell: located in the east of Gold Hill.
* screen: a curtain which separates or cuts off, shelters or protects as a light partition, a common image in Chinese literature. A poem in *The Book of Songs* reads like this: "You wait for me before the screen; / Your hat-rings white do tinkle clean, / And your rubies brilliantly sheen."
* Lord Glee: the court title of Lingyün Hsieh (A.D. 385 – A.D. 433), a highborn poet, official, idyllist, Buddhist and traveler, famous for landscape poems in particular.
* Ch'in: the Ch'in State or the State of Ch'in (770 B.C – 221 B.C.); the first unified regime of China, i.e. the Ch'in Empire (221 B.C.– 207 B.C.).
* mulberry: the edible, berry-like fruit of a tree (genus *Morus*) whose leaves are valued for silkworm culture, and the tree itself, first cultivated in the drainage area of the Yellow River in China about five thousand years ago.

客 中 作

兰陵美酒郁金香，
玉碗盛来琥珀光。
但使主人能醉客，
不知何处是他乡。

Away from Home

Of turmeric smells the Orchid Hill Wine;
Like amber the jadeite cup filled does shine.
If my host can make me drunk, drunk a lot,
I don't care whether it's my home or not.

* turmeric: a widely cultivated tropical plant of India having yellow flowers and a large aromatic deep yellow rhizome; source of a condiment and a yellow dye.
* the Orchid Hill: an ancient town in present-day Orchid Hill, Lin-e, Shantung Province, so named because it was close to a knoll lush with orchids. In 255 B.C. invited by the prime minister of Ch'u, Hsüntzu (313 B.C.- 238 B.C.) became as its magistrate and served for 20 years.
* amber: a yellow or brownish-yellow translucent fossil resin found along some seacoasts and used in jewelry, pipe-stems etc.

太 原 早 秋

岁落众芳歇，
时当大火流。
霜威出塞早，
云色渡河秋。
梦绕边城月，
心飞故国楼。
思归若汾水，
无日不悠悠。

Early Autumn in Great Plain

The autumn falling, blooms retire;
Now you still feel you are on fire.
There falls frost from the north pass then;
Clouds tinge autumn across the Fen.
My dream lingers with the town's moon;
My heart is urged to go home soon.
Just like the Fen, my missing goes;
Day in and day out, there it flows.

* Great Plain: referring to T'aiyüan if transliterated, the place where the first emperor of T'ang, Yüan Li, and the second emperor, Shihmin Li, i.e. Yüan Li's son, were stationed in the Sui dynasty. As Great Plain was once called T'ang, T'ang was adopted as the name of the T'ang Empire.
* the moon: the celestial body that revolves around the earth from west to east as a satellite, which appears at night and gives off shining silvery light, an image of purity and solitude in Chinese culture.
* the Fen: the River Fen, the second largest branch of the Yellow River.

奔亡道中五首

Fleeing on the Way, Five Poems

其　一

苏武天山上，
田横海岛边。
万重关塞断，
何日是归年？

No. 1

Exiled to north border was Su;
T'ien fled to an isle in the blue.
All passes have been blocked like so;
When can I go home? I don't know.

* Su: referring to Wu Su (140 B.C.- 60 B.C.), a minister of Han. On his diplomatic mission, Su was detained in the west. The Huns tried to make him surrender with threats and promises, only to fail. Then, he was sent to North Sea to be a shepherd. Through all kinds of hardship, Su finally came back to Han after 19 years' detention, during which time, Wu Su had never surrendered.
* T'ien: referring to Heng T'ien, a chief of an uprising at the end of Ch'in. T'ien rejected Pang Liu's offer of amnesty and committed suicide at Firstshine. His five hundred followers drowned themselves when hearing the news.

其 二

亭伯去安在？
李陵降未归。
愁容变海色，
短服改胡衣。

No. 2

Where is T'ingpo, o where is he?
Ling surrendered but ceased to be.
My grimace a sea blue does don;
No more Han coats, Hun style takes on.

* T'ingpo: referring to Yin Ts'ui (? – A.D. 92), T'ingpo being his courtesy name. Ts'ui could not bear his irritable superior and resigned.
* Ling: referring to Ridge Li (134 B.C.- 74 B.C.), a renowned commander in the Han dynasty. He surrendered after a fierce battle against the Huns. However, Emperor Martial believed a rumor about Ling and killed his family, which cut off all the connection between Ling and Han. After that, Ling stayed with the Huns.
* Hun: nomadic Asians west and north of China in ancient times.

其 三

谈笑三军却，
交游七贵疏。
仍留一只箭，
未射鲁连书。

No. 3

While laughing, I scare foes to flee,
Howe'er, the peers have estranged me.
With one arrow, I keep about;
One day I'll shoot the letter out.

* the letter: an allusion to Lien Lu's letter. As is recorded in history, Lien Lu (305 B.C.-245 B.C.), i.e. Chunglien Lu, a famous strategist in the Warring States period, shot a letter into Liao, a town occupied by Way troops, and when the Way general read the letter he killed himself due to his anxiety and apprehension caused by the letter, so Liao was taken easily by Ch'i's army. A letter can kill a general and take a town, which is a case of winning a war without fighting.

其　四

函谷如玉关，
几时可生还？
洛阳为易水，
嵩岳是燕山。
俗变羌胡语，
人多沙塞颜。
申包惟恸哭，
七日鬓毛斑。

No. 4

Like Jade Gate blocked is Case Dale Pass;
Could I go back alive? Alas!
Like the Change, the Lo has got blocked;
Like Mt. Yan, Mt. Tower has been rocked.
Our speech is replaced by Huns' tongue;
Here and there alien faces throng.
In vain Paohsu Shen wailed all day,
In seven days, his hair grew gray.

* Jade Gate: an important military fort and passage on the Great Wall, built in the Han dynasty, located in the north of today's Tunhuang, Kansu Province. As is recorded, to guard against Hun invasions, Emperor Martial of Han formed alliance with nations in the western regions to initiate the route between east and west, and instituted four sires and built two passes with beacons west of the Yellow River. Fortresses were made from Lingchü to Wine Spring in 111 B.C. and more fortresses made from Wine Spring to Jade Gate.
* Case Dale Pass: an ancient pass located to the east of the capital of T'ang, and Lint'ao to the west.

* the Change: referring to the River Change, by which Chingk'e bade farewell to his lord and friend, and set off for his mission.
* Mt. Yan: one of the most famous mountains in Northern China, rolling from Changchiak'ou to Mountain-sea Pass, 420 kilometers long, 200 kilometers wide at most.
* Mt. Tower: one of the Five Mountains in China, located in Honan Province, along with Mt. Ever in Shanhsi, Mt. Arch in Shantung, Mt. Flora in Sha'anhsi, and Mt. Scale in Hunan.
* Paohsü Shen: a senior official of Ch'u in the Spring and Autumn period. In order to revive his motherland, Shen went to Ch'in and cried for seven days to ask for help which moved the lord and officials in Ch'in.

其 五

森森望湖水，
青青芦叶齐。
归心落何处，
日没大江西。
歇马傍春草，
欲行远道迷。
谁忍子规鸟，
连声向我啼。

No. 5

The Hsiang stretches on and does flow;
The reeds so green side by side grow.
Where can my heart go, where to run?
West of the river sinks the sun.
I'd rest my horse now by spring grass;
It's a long way! I've lost the pass.
Who can bear that cuckoo's sad cry?
It shrieks to me, who can but sigh.

* the Hsiang: a river in Hunan, the major source of Lake Cavehall.
* horse: a large herbivorous solid-hoofed quadruped (*Equus caballus*) with a coarse mane and tail, of various strains: Ferghana, Mongolian, Kazaks, Hequ, Karasahr and so on, and of various colors: black, white, yellow, brown, dappled and so on, commonly in the domesticated state, employed as a beast of draught and burden and especially for riding upon.
* cuckoo: any of a family of birds with a long, slender body, grayish-brown on top and white below, a symbol of sadness in Chinese culture. As is said, during the Shang

dynasty, Cuckoo (Yü Tu), a caring king of Shu, abdicated the throne due to a flood and lived in reclusion. After his death, he turned into a cuckoo, wailing day and night, shedding tears and blood.

郢门秋怀

郢门一为客,
巴月三成弦。
朔风正摇落,
行子愁归旋。
杳杳山外日,
茫茫江上天。
人迷洞庭水,
雁度潇湘烟。
清旷谐宿好,
缁磷及此年。
百龄何荡漾,
万化相推迁。
空谒苍梧帝,
徒寻溟海仙。
已闻蓬海浅,
岂见三桃圆。
倚剑增浩叹,
扪襟还自怜。
终当游五湖,
濯足沧浪泉。

Touched by Autumn in Ying Gate

In Ying Gate for a month I've been;
The moon's changed thrice, glow, shine, or sheen.
The north wind and the leaves both sough;

A vagrant, I am homesick now.
Beyond the mountain sets the sun;
The sky vast, I'm a lonely one.
Lake Cavehall rolls on like a maze;
Wild geese return throughout the haze.
For practice, it's a calm good lot;
For years, my pursuit has changed not.
One hundred years ripple so fast;
Turns after turns continue to last.
Lord Hibiscus I've failed to see,
And where is Sea God, where is he?
Fairy Sea's turned shallow, as known;
The peaches have thrice ripely grown.
My sword, caressed, heaves a long sigh;
I pommel my chest to the sky.
To lakes and seas I would retreat
And in the blue waves wash my feet.

* Ying Gate: referring to Chaste Gate, an important town in all dynasties.
* Lake Cavehall: a lake in present-day Hunan Province.
* wild goose: an undomesticated goose that is caring and responsible, taken as a symbol of benevolence, righteousness, good manner, wisdom, and faith in Chinese culture.
* Lord Hibiscus: Shun if transliterated, an ancient sovereign, a descendant of Lord Yellow, regarded as one of Five Lords in prehistoric China.
* Sea God: the sovereign of all seas.
* Fairy Sea: the sea where there are Fairy Isles where immortals abide.
* peach: any tree of the genus *Prunus Percica*, blooming brilliantly and bearing fruit, a fleshy, juicy, edible drupe, considered sacred in China, a symbol of romance, prosperity and longevity.
* To lakes and seas I would retreat: In Pai Li one may find an escapist. Once he was frustrated, he would retreat to reclusion where he could see infinitely more in the universe than what was worrying him.

至鸭栏驿上白马矶赠裴侍御

侧叠万古石，
横为白马矶。
乱流若电转，
举棹扬珠辉。
临驿卷绨幕，
升堂接绣衣。
情亲不避马，
为我解霜威。

To P'ei, the Royal Servant, at White Horse Stack at Duck Pen Post

The age-old stones ashore, a stack,
Look like a white horse shining crack.
The splash gives a lightning roar;
Drops or foams jump up from the oar.
In the hall, up is the screen drawn;
There you offer me a silk gown.
You keep me close as your friend dear,
And get me off the frost severe.

* White Horse Stack: a rock protrusion near Duck Pen Post in today's Hillshine, Hunan Province.
* Duck Pen Post: a post or station 7.5 kilometers from Linhsiang County, in today's Hillshine, Hunan Province.
* screen: a curtain which separates or cuts off, shelters or protects as a light partition, a

common image in Chinese literature. Two lines from a Sung lyric by Haowen Yüan reads like this:"The drizzle falls before my tower's sill; / 'Broidered with crabapples, the screen's chill."

荆门浮舟望蜀江

春水月峡来，
浮舟望安极？
正是桃花流，
依然锦江色。
江色绿且明，
茫茫与天平。
逶迤巴山尽，
摇曳楚云行。
雪照聚沙雁，
花飞出谷莺。
芳洲却已转，
碧树森森迎。
流目浦烟夕，
扬帆海月生。
江陵识遥火，
应到渚宫城。

Looking at the Shu River While Boating in Chastegate

Past Moon Gorge spring water does flow;
Gazing afar, my boat I row.
Behold, the peach blossoms flow down,
Like the Silk Stream in my hometown.
The greenness of the river surges
And o'er there with the skyline merges.

The Pa Hills undulate their way;
With the clouds over Ch'u they sway.
The wild geese take a bath ashore;
The orioles o'er the valley soar.
The shoal turns off, which I don't meet;
But the forest there does me greet.
The mist on the stream meets my eyes;
The moon and the sail both arise.
Lo, the wall's with lanterns alive,
Shoalton is there—I'll soon arrive.

* the Shu River: originating from Mt. Min, flowing to Shu.
* Chastegate: located on the southern bank of the Yangtze River, Hupei.
* Moon Gorge: a gorge Pa County, the main urban area of today's Double Gain (Ch'ungch'ing).
* peach: any of the plant (*Prunus Percica*), bearing a fleshy, juicy, edible drupe, cultivated in many varieties in temperate zones considered sacred in China, often used as a metaphor for a young woman, as a section of a poem in *The Book of Songs* reads: "The peach twigs sway, / Ablaze the flower; / Now she's married away, / Befitting her new bower."
* the Silk Stream: a stretch of river in Ch'engtu.
* wild goose: an undomesticated goose that is caring and responsible, taken as a symbol of benevolence, righteousness, good manner, wisdom, and faith in Chinese culture.
* Shoalton: a resort built by a king of Ch'u in the Spring and Autumn period.

上 三 峡

巫山夹青天，
巴水流若兹。
巴水忽可尽，
青天无到时。
三朝上黄牛，
三暮行太迟。
三朝又三暮，
不觉鬓成丝。

Rowing in Three Gorges

Mt. Witch the blue sky would fain kiss;
The Pa River flows, flows like this.
The Pa River comes to an end;
The blue sky does still there suspend.
Three morns in Yellow Ox I row;
Three evens I'm still there, too slow.
Three morns and three evens I go;
Unawares, some gray hairs I grow.

* Three Gorges: referring to the three gorges of the Long River, that is, Big Pond Gorge, Witch Gorge, and Westridge Gorge.
* Mt. Witch: a mythical and religious mountain, which was thought to be a range of mountains in Sha'anhsi.
* the Pa River: the part of the Long River in the State of Pa, the capital of which is Riverton, today's Ch'ungch'ing.
* Yellow Ox: a gorge of the Long River.

自巴东舟行经瞿唐峡登巫山最高峰晚还题壁

江行几千里,
海月十五圆。
始经瞿唐峡,
遂步巫山巅。
巫山高不穷,
巴国尽所历。
日边攀垂萝,
霞外倚穹石。
飞步凌绝顶,
极目无纤烟。
却顾失丹壑,
仰观临青天。
青天若可扪,
银汉去安在?
望云知苍梧,
记水辨瀛海。
周游孤光晚,
历览幽意多。
积雪照空谷,
悲风鸣森柯。
归途行欲曛,
佳趣尚未歇,
江寒早啼猿,
松暝已吐月。
月色何悠悠,
清猿响啾啾。

辞山不忍听，

挥策还孤舟。

Boating from East Pa via Big Pond Gorge, Climbing Mt. Witch and Writing an Inscription on a Cliff When Coming Back at Dusk

Thousands of miles downstream I row;

The fifteenth sees the round moon glow.

At first, Big Pond I row through;

Then I climb up Mt. Witch to view.

All o'er the State of Pa I've been;

Mt. Witch's too high, the mountains green.

Near the sun I hold to a vine;

Out the clouds, on a crag recline.

I run up to the very height;

There's not any cloud within sight.

Glancing back, I find the dale gone;

Looking up, I see clouds hang on.

If the sky you can touch up there?

Where is the Milky Way, o where?

Head raised, Mt. Hibiscus you'll see;

Stream chased, in the ocean you'll be.

Till dusk falls I tour all around;

Still there many sights to be found.

The snow thick to the valley shines;

The wind sad to the forest whines.

It's dusk when I'm on my way back;

I'm still in high spirits, not slack.

The river cold hears monkeys cry;

> The pines dark face the moon on high.
> How Luna turns out pale and bleak!
> How monkeys there so sadly shriek!
> I'll go, such cries I cannot bear;
> I make haste to find my boat there.

* Big Pond Gorge: one of the three gorges of the Long River.
* Mt. Witch: a mythical and religious mountain, which was thought to be a range of mountains in Sha'anhsi.
* the moon: the planet of the earth, which appears at night and gives off shining silvery light. It has various associations in Chinese culture, for example, purity, solitude, nostalgia, or happy reunion when it is round on the fifteenth night.
* the State of Pa: a state in the upper reaches of the Long River in the southwest of China. The state was formed in 11th century B.C. and expired in 316 B.C.
* the Milky Way: a luminous band circling the heavens composed of stars and nebulae; the Galaxy.
* Mt. Hibiscus: referring to Mt. Nine Doubts where Lord Hibiscus was buried.

早发白帝城

朝辞白帝彩云间，
千里江陵一日还。
两岸猿声啼不住，
轻舟已过万重山。

Early Departure from Whitegod

I leave Whitegod mid clouds hued by the sun;
Three hundred miles to Chaste is one day's run.
The apes ashore can't stop me with their shrills;
The skiff downstream passes ten thousand hills.

* Whitegod: an ancient city founded in A.D. 25 at the end of the Western Han dynasty (202 B.C. - A.D. 8), located at Mt. Whitegod, near present-day Double Gain (Ch'ungch'ing). Shu Lordson heard that there was a well called White Crane in the town, wherefrom white mist in the shape of a dragon often rose to the sky, and he regarded it as a symbol of his ascension to the throne, so he crowned himself as White God or White Emperor. And it is famous in history as the place where Pei Liu, the Emperor of Shu, died in the Three Kingdoms Period (A.D. 220 - A.D. 280). It is famous in history as the place where Pei Liu, the Emperor of Shu, died in the Three Kingdoms Period (A.D. 220 - A.D. 280).
* Chaste: a geographical region including areas of present-day Hupei and Hunan.
* skiff: a light rowboat for fishing or lotus-picking and so on; formerly a sailing vessel.

秋 下 荆 门

霜落荆门江树空，
布帆无恙挂秋风。
此行不为鲈鱼鲙，
自爱名山入剡中。

Leaving Shu for Mt. Chastegate in Autumn

Frost whitens Chastegate, riverside trees bare;
Before autumn wind the sail's free of care.
This trip is not for a taste of perches,
But the mountains' charm my mind bewitches.

* Shu: one of the earliest kingdoms in China, founded by Silkworm according to legend. In the Three Kingdoms period, a new Shu was established by Pei Liu, hence one of the three kingdoms in that period.
* Chastegate: Chingmen if transliterated, an important city in today's Hupei Province, located on the southern bank of the Long River, Hupei.

江 行 寄 远

刳木出吴楚，
危槎百馀尺。
疾风吹片帆，
日暮千里隔。
别时酒犹在，
已为异乡客。
思君不可得，
愁见江水碧。

To My Friend When I Row on the River

A thirty-meter-long canoe
I row ahead to Wu and Ch'u.
The high wind to the sail does blow;
One day three hundred miles I go.
So drunk when biding you adieu,
Now I'm in a strange land you know.
Just one day I start to miss you,
The blue river fills me with woe.

* Wu: the State of Wu (12th century B.C.- 473 B.C.), a vassal state in the lower reaches of the Long River, annexed by the State of Yüeh.
* Ch'u: a vassal state of Chough, one of the powers in the Warring States period, conquered and annexed by Ch'in in 223 B.C., covering the regions of present-day Hunan, Hupei and neighboring areas.

宿五松山下荀媪家

我宿五松下，
寂寥无所欢。
田家秋作苦，
邻女夜舂寒。
跪进雕胡饭，
月光明素盘。
令人惭漂母，
三谢不能餐。

Putting Up at Mother Hsun's at the Foot of Mt. Five Pines

In Five Pines I stay for the night;
Lonely, nothing there can me thrill.
The peasants, hard, remain in plight;
A neighbor husks in the night chill.
My hostess cooks waterweed seed;
The moon lights up her plate of rice.
Washing Mum, ashamed of your need,
I won't eat and I decline thrice.

* Mt. Five Pines: located in T'ungling, Anhui, so named because there grew five pines on the very top. According to *Geographical Wonders* compiled in the Southern Sung dynasty, "The mountain boasted old pines, five in one, a pentad, reaching high to the sky with scale-like bark on the trunk."
* waterweed seed: seed from an edible plant called wild rice, what is zizania aquatica in Latin, a food Chinese have eaten for thousands of years, now esteemed as a table

delicacy.

* Washing Mum: an allusion to Washing Mother, the laundry lady who provided Hsin Han with food when the later commander was poor.

下泾县陵阳溪至涩滩

涩滩鸣嘈嘈,
两山足猿猱。
白波若卷雪,
侧足不容舠。
渔子与舟人,
撑折万张篙。

From the Ridgeshine Stream in Ching County to Hard Sands

Hard Sands gurgles and gurgles on;
On the two mountains monkeys run.
The white waves are thrown up like snow;
The boulder there bars my canoe.
A boatman, for a boatman's sake,
A year will ten thousand sprits break.

* the Ridgeshine Stream: a stream dangerous with rocks in Ridgeshine County in present-day Anhui Province. As legend goes, Sir Glare became immortal on his way to a mountain in Ridgeshine.
* Ching County: a county of State Pacifier Prefecture, in today's Anhui Province.
* Hard Sands: a shoal full of grotesque rocks located in today's Ching County, Anhui Province.

下陵阳沿高溪三门六刺滩

三门横峻滩，
六刺走波澜。
石惊虎伏起，
水状龙萦盘。
何惭七里濑，
使我欲垂竿。

From Ridgeshine to Three Gates and Six Pricks on the High Stream

Three gates stand before Harsh Sands;
Six Pricks like stabs, water expands.
The rock's like a tiger that lies;
The surge's like a dragon that flies.
Seven Miles can't with this compare;
I would go fishing here for e'er.

* Ridgeshine: Lingyang if transliterated, a county located in present-day Anhui Province. As legend goes, Sir Glare became immortal on his way to Mt. Ridgeshine.
* Harsh Sands: name of a shoal formed with sand.
* Six Pricks: name of a beach with six dangerous shoals in the Ridgeshine Stream in today's Ching County, Anhui Province.
* dragon: a fabulous serpent-like giant winged animal that can change its girth and length, a totem of the Chinese nation, a symbol of benevolence and sovereignty in Chinese culture.
* Seven Miles: referring to Seven-Mile Rapids located in today's T'unglu, Chechiang Province.

夜泊黄山闻殷十四吴吟

昨夜谁为吴会吟，
风生万壑振空林。
龙惊不敢水中卧，
猿啸时闻岩下音。
我宿黄山碧溪月，
听之却罢松间琴。
朝来果是沧洲逸，
酤酒醍盘饭霜栗。
半酣更发江海声，
客愁顿向杯中失。

Hearing Wu Fourteen Chanting a Song of Wu When I Put Up for the Night at Mt. Yellow

Last night who chanted there a song of Wu,
Like wind rose from vales and to the wood blew?
The dragon's scared and lies in water still;
The monkey howls and neath stone hears a trill.
By Mt. Yellow's moonlit stream I stay,
And in the pines I stop the lute I play.
At dawn I find you're a hermit indeed,
So I take wine and chestnuts to you feed.
I roar and shout out a song while half drunk,
So my worries are in my cup made sunk.

* Wu: the place that was the vassal state of Wu, now referring to the southern land of

China, usually the area before south of the Yangtze River.
* dragon: a fabulous serpent-like giant winged animal, a symbol of benevolence and sovereignty in Chinese culture.
* Mt. Yellow: located in Anhui Province, one of the most famous mountains in China with natural, literary and cultural attractions, featured with wondrous pines, clouds and hotsprings. It's said that Lord Yellow (2717 B.C.- 2599 B.C.) used to make elixirs here, hence Yellow.
* chestnut: a smooth shelled, sweet, edible nut of any of the genus (*Castanea*) of trees of the beech family, growing in a prickly bur.

宿鰕湖

鸡鸣发黄山，
暝投鰕湖宿。
白雨映寒山，
森森似银竹。
提携采铅客，
结荷水边沐。
半夜四天开，
星河烂人目。
明晨大楼去，
岗陇多屈伏。
当与持斧翁，
前溪伐云木。

Put Up for the Night on Lake Shrimp

I leave Mt. Yellow at day break,
And as dusk falls I reach Shrimp Lake.
The white rain pours to the hills cold;
Like white rods is the downpour bold.
I follow lead miners, with whom
I bathe by lotuses in bloom.
Then it stops raining at midnight;
The Milky Way dazzlingly bright.
I'm leaving for Mt. Tower at dawn;
The hills meander up and down.
The chopper comes along to me;

We will by the stream fell the tree.

* Lake Shrimp: a lake near Mt. Yellow in today's Anhui Province, named after numerous diminutive, long-tailed, crustaceans (genus *Crago*).
* Mt. Yellow: located in Anhui Province, one of the most famous mountains in China with natural, literary and cultural attractions, featured with wondrous pines, clouds and hotsprings. It's said that Lord Yellow, one of the fathers of Chinese civilization, used to make elixirs here.
* the Milky Way: the Silver River in Chinese mythology, a luminous band circling the heavens composed of stars and nebulae; the Galaxy.
* Mt. Tower: one of the five famous mountains in China, famous for Youngwood (Shaolin) Temple and its Buddhist martial arts.

西 施

西施越溪女，
出自苎萝山。
秀色掩今古，
荷花羞玉颜。
浣纱弄碧水，
自与清波闲。
皓齿信难开，
沉吟碧云间。
勾践徵绝艳，
扬蛾入吴关。
提携馆娃宫，
杳渺讵可攀。
一破夫差国，
千秋竟不还。

West Maid

West Maid did bathe in the Yüeh Stream;
She came from Mt. Gaudish so high.
She faded beauties with her gleam;
Before her lotuses felt shy.
She washed yarn in water blue,
Free of care like the ripples there.
Her pearly teeth she did not show
But singing amid clouds so fair.
King Kouchien recruited girls best;

Raising her brows, she went to Wu.
She was led to House Babe to rest;
How she felt o'er there no one knew.
When Wu perished under attack,
Never ever did she come back.

* West Maid: once a laundry lady in the State of Yüeh which was then a tributary to the State of Wu. Because of her beauty, West Maid was selected to be trained in Yüeh's palace, and sent to the King of Wu as a spy. She quickly won the king's affection, with her irresistible charm. As a result, the State of Wu waned and perished.
* Mt. Gaudish: 2.5 kilometers from Chuch'i, where Maid West lived, in present-day Chechiang Province.
* King Kouchien: King Kouchien of Yüeh (520 B.C.- 465 B.C.), successfully wiped out the State of Wu for revenge, and burnt Wu's Palace around 473 B.C.
* House Babe: a palace Kouchien built for West Maid.

王 右 军

右军本清真，
潇洒出风尘。
山阴过羽客，
爱此好鹅宾。
扫素写道经，
笔精妙入神。
书罢笼鹅去，
何曾别主人。

Right General Wang

Right General was true and upright;
He was aloft there on the height.
He was a hermit plumed at ease
And tenderly he loved white geese.
The Word and the World copied he;
So obsessed in profundity.
He caged the goose, the verse finished;
The bird from him never vanished.

* Right General: one of the four kinds of generals named with directions in Chinese history: Left General, Right General, Front General and Rear General, which are first-ranking generals or marshals.
* Right General Wang: referring to Hsichih Wang (A.D. 303 – A.D. 379), a high ranking official and general and the most famous highborn calligrapher in the Eastern Chin dynasty, regarded as the Sage of Handwriting.
* *The Word and the World*: the foundational classic of Wordism, written by Laocius

(471 B.C.-571 B.C.), a great philosopher in the Spring and Autumn period. It is the single book that Laocius wrote all his wisdom into.
* goose: one of a subfamily (*Anserinae*) of wild or domesticated web-footed birds larger than ducks and smaller than swans, usually a sign of good luck because of its red protruding head.

上 元 夫 人

上元谁夫人？
偏得王母娇。
嵯峨三角髻，
馀发散垂腰。
裘披青毛锦，
身著赤霜袍。
手提嬴女儿，
闲与凤吹箫。
眉语两自笑，
忽然随风飘。

Lady Up

Who's Lady Up, the One on high?
From Queen Mother she's love and care.
Her bun is like a mountain high,
And onto her waist droops her hair.
She wears fur with plumes shining grand,
Which with her red coat makes a suit.
With Music Fairy hand in hand,
She to the phoenix plays the flute.
They laugh, and each to each they smile;
They are gone, having stayed a while!

* Lady Up: a fairy in Chinese mythology, the youngest daughter of Queen Mother.
* Queen Mother: referring to Mother West, a sovereign goddess living on Mt. Queen in

Chinese myths. She was originally described as human-bodied, tiger-toothed, leopard-tailed and hoopoe-haired, regarded as a goddess in charge of women protection, marriage and procreation, and longevity. According to *Sir Lush*, with the Word, Queen Mother sat on Mt. Young Broad.

* Music Fairy: Lord Solemn of Ch'in's daughter, who was good at music, especially good at zither playing.
* phoenix: In Chinese myths, phoenixes, auspicious birds, unlike ordinary ones, only perch on parasol trees, and only eat bamboo shoots and pearly stone.

苏 台 览 古

旧苑荒台杨柳新，
菱歌清唱不胜春。
只今惟有西江月，
曾照吴王宫里人。

Visiting Kusu Mound

The willows wave on the old court and mound;
The Water Chestnut song lures spring around.
West of the river shines the moon so fair;
It used to gleam those in the palace there.

* Kusu Mound: a palace built by King Fuch'ai of Wu (cir. 528 B.C.- 473 B.C.) to please West Maid.
* willow: any of a large genus of shrubs and trees related to the poplars, having generally smooth branches, and often long, slender, pliant, and sometimes pendent branchlets, a symbol of farewell or nostalgia in Chinese culture. The best image is in *Vetch We Pick*, a verse in *The Book of Songs*, which reads like this: When we left long ago, / The willows waved adieu. / Now back to our home town, / We meet snow falling down.
* *The Water Chestnut*: a folk song usually sung while water chestnuts are gathered.
* the moon: the celestial body that revolves around the earth from west to east as a satellite, which appears at night and gives off shining silvery light, an image of purity and solitude in Chinese culture.

越中览古

越王勾践破吴归,
义士还家尽锦衣。
宫女如花满春殿,
只今惟有鹧鸪飞。

Visiting the Relics in Yüeh

King Kouchien did King of Wu terminate;
His army men came back in clothes ornate.
The court maids tripped about like blossoms gay;
But only partridges fly o'er there today.

* Yüeh: the State of Yüeh (2032 B.C.- 222 B.C.), a vassal state in Southeast China through the ages of Hsia, Shang, and Chough.
* King Kouchien: King Kouchien of Yüeh (520 B.C.- 465 B.C.), who successfully wiped out the State of Wu for revenge, and burnt Wu's Palace around 473 B.C.
* King of Wu: referring to King Fuch'ai of Wu (cir. 528 B.C.- 473 B.C.), who committed suicide when his state was to expire.
* partridge: a kind of small, plump-bodied gallinaceous game bird, having white spots on the chest, a symbol of lovesickness in Chinese culture, as it utters a plaintive cry sounding like: "bro-bro, no-go-go".

商 山 四 皓

白发四老人，
昂藏南山侧。
偃卧松雪间，
冥翳不可识。
云窗拂青霭，
石壁横翠色。
龙虎方战争，
于焉自休息。
秦人失金镜，
汉祖升紫极。
阴虹浊太阳，
前星遂沦匿。
一行佐明圣，
倏起生羽翼。
功成身不居，
舒卷在胸臆。
窅冥合元化，
茫昧信难测。
飞声塞天衢，
万古仰遗则。

The Four Old Men at Mt. Shang

The four old men growing white hair,
Raised up, lived in the South Hills there.
They lay in pines so thick with snow;

Their whereabouts no one did know.
To their cloud windows haze did fall;
And green climbed onto the stone wall.
Dragons and tigers fought outside;
They stayed here, and here did abide.
The Ch'in Empire was beaten down;
Highsire came to power in his crown.
The sun was eclipsed with a shade;
The star would fall, all but sunk made.
They came downhill to help the throne;
The fledgling would be fully grown.
Upon success they did retire;
They had an aim aloft, much higher.
With the great Word they would unite,
Abstruse to the world without light.
They fly o'er Heaven's Thoroughfare,
To be worshiped and loved fore'er.

* the Four Old Men at Mt. Shang: referring to four Wordist hermits living in reclusion at Mt. Shang. They were invited as a think tank for the House of Han in the 3rd century B.C. They withdrew from the world at the end of the reign of Emperor First of Ch'in and were welcomed and venerated by the new emperor of Han.
* the South Hills: referring to Mt. Shang in this poem.
* the Ch'in Empire: the Ch'in State or the State of Ch'in (905 B.C.- 221 B.C.), enfeoffed as a dependency of Chough by King Piety of Chough in 905 B.C. and enfeoffed as a vassal state by King Peace of Chough in 770 B.C. In the ten years from 230 B.C. to 221 B.C., Ch'in wiped out the other six powers and became the first unified regime of China, i.e. the Ch'in Empire.
* the great Word: the Word, the highest existence in the universe, the Creator of all things.

过四皓墓

我行至商洛，
幽独访神仙。
园绮复安在？
云萝尚宛然。
荒凉千古迹，
芜没四坟连。
伊昔炼金鼎，
何年闭玉泉？
陇寒惟有月，
松古渐无烟。
木魅风号去，
山精雨啸旋。
紫芝高咏罢，
青史旧名传。
今日并如此，
哀哉信可怜。

The Tombs of the Four Old Men

The Lo I wade; the Shang I climb;
I'd see the saints in this quiet clime.
Where are the saints, o where are they;
The luxuriant vines sprawl their way.
It's such a desolate old place;
The four tombs sit there face to face.
Then in here elixir they made;

When did they close the Spring of Jade?
The mounts cold see the moon cold shine;
No leaves old stay on the old pine.
Demons and devils rise to wail,
In the wind hurled with rain and hail.
Song of Ganoderma's now gone,
But their names will be carried on.
Today's world is just like the past;
History's a cycle turning fast!

* the Four Old Men: referring to four Wordist hermits living in reclusion at Mt. Shang. They were invited as imperial advisors, a think tank for the House of Han in the 3rd century B.C. They withdrew from the world at the end of the reign of Emperor First of Ch'in and were welcomed and venerated by the new emperor of Han.
* the Lo: the Lo River, which flows through Loshine.
* the Shang: Mt. Shang, the southern hills that the Four Old Men dwelled.
* the Spring of Jade: a metaphor for a spring with its source deep underground.
* *Song of Ganoderma*: a song composed by the Four Old Men.

岘山怀古

访古登岘首,
凭高眺襄中。
天清远峰出,
水落寒沙空。
弄珠见游女,
醉酒怀山公。
感叹发秋兴,
长松鸣夜风。

Visiting an Old Sight on Mt. Steep

I climb Mt. Steep for an old sight,
And o'erlook Sowshine on the height.
It's fine, and far-off peaks unfold;
The stream so low, the shoal looks cold.
I see the girl kiss the pearl's shine;
I miss Hillman now drunk with wine.
I sigh long at the autumn now;
The pine to the night wind does sough.

* Mt. Steep: an important fort in history, located in the southwest of Sowshine (Hsiangyang), with the River Han to its east. There are many literary works about Mt. Steep.
* Sowshine: referring to Hsiangyang if transliterated, an important city in today's Hupei Province.
* pearl: a smooth, lustrous, usually white and bluish-gray, calcareous concretion deposited in layers around a central nucleus in the shells of various mollusks or oysters,

and largely used as a gem, medicine or given as a gift, a metaphor for the dearest one, a representation of nobility, purity and dignity in Chinese culture.

* Hillman: Chien Shan (A.D. 253 - A.D. 312), a celebrity and general in the Chin dynasty, the fifth son of T'ao Shan, one of the Seven Sages of the Bamboo Grove. He was as gentle and graceful as his father. When he was an official, the nation was falling apart and other officials were worried and depressed. Hillman, however, lived a casual life. When he hanged out, he used to hold a banquet and get drunk at the High Sun Pool.

苏　武

苏武在匈奴，
十年持汉节。
白雁上林飞，
空传一书札。
牧羊边地苦，
落日归心绝。
渴饮月窟冰，
饥餐天上雪。
东还沙塞远，
北怆河梁别。
泣把李陵衣，
相看泪成血。

Wu Su

Wu Su was kept in Alien Land;
For ten years loyal he did stand.
The wild goose flew to send his word
To Lord Martial, the greatest Lord.
On the border he tended sheep;
The setting sun saw his heart weep.
If thirsty, he drank hoarded ice;
When hungry, he ate snow as rice.
When he was going back to the east,
He couldn't start off, not the least.
Out crying, he took Ridge Li's sleeve,

His tears in blood, he did there grieve.

* Wu Su: Wu Su (140 B.C.- 60 B.C.), a minister of Han. On his diplomatic mission, Su was detained. The Huns tried to make him surrender with threats and promises, only to fail. Then, he was sent to North Sea, i.e., today's Lake Baikal to be a shepherd. Through all kinds of hardship, Su finally came back to Han after 19 years' detention, during which time, Wu Su had never surrendered.
* Alien Land: referring to the Huns' land.
* wild goose: an undomesticated goose that is caring and responsible, taken as a symbol of benevolence, righteousness, good manner, wisdom, and faith in Chinese culture.
* Lord Martial: referring to Emperor Martial of Han.
* sheep: a medium-sized domesticated ruminant of the genus *Ovis*, highly prized for its flesh, wool and skin, regarded as meek and mild, a symbol of beauty and purity, used as a sacrifice in both Western and Eastern cultures.
* Ridge Li: Ling Li (134 B.C.- 74 B.C.), a renowned commander in the Han dynasty. He surrendered after a fierce battle against the Huns. However, Emperor Martial believed a rumor about Ling and killed his families which cut off all the connection between Ling and Han. After that, Ling stayed with the Huns.

经下邳圯桥怀张子房

子房未虎啸,
破产不为家。
沧海得壮士,
椎秦博浪沙。
报韩虽不成,
天地皆振动。
潜匿游下邳,
岂曰非智勇?
我来圯桥上,
怀古钦英风。
唯见碧流水,
曾无黄石公。
叹息此人去,
萧条徐泗空。

Thinking of Tsefang on the Bridge in Hsiap'i

When Tsefang did not have his day,
For an assassin all he'd pay.
From Blue Sea he got a strong hand,
Who sniped the tyrant at Wave Sand.
Though in this attempt he did fail,
Both Heaven and earth quaked to hail.
He fled to Hsiap'i and there hid;
Is that not something brave he did?

I come to the bridge and look higher,
His great bravery I do admire.
Here but the water flows alone,
Where is the old man, Yellow Stone?
On this bridge here I can but sigh;
Now Hsu or Ssu is bare and dry.

* Tsefang: the courtesy name of Liang Chang (250 B.C.- 186 B.C.), a prominent statesman and counsellor, and one of the founders of Han. In Hsiap'i, he met Yellow Stone, a legendary Wordist, and got *The Art of War* from him.
* Hsiap'i: a place tracing back to the Warring State period, a fief, then the capital of a prefecture early in the Han dynasty, a vassal state enfeoffed to Hsin Han in 202 B.C. and a kingdom in the Emperor Bright of Han's reign, a place of strategic importance.
* Blue Sea: the changing world in general.
* Wave Sand: the place where Liang Chang attempted to assassinate Emperor First.
* Yellow Stone: an old legendary Wordist, who gave Liang Chang the strategist *The Art of War*.
* Hsu or Ssu: referring to Hsuchow and the Ssu River, in present-day Chiangsu Province.

金陵三首

Gold Hill, Three Poems

其 一

晋家南渡日，
此地旧长安。
地即帝王宅，
山为龙虎盘。
金陵空壮观，
天堑净波澜。
醉客回桡去，
吴歌且自欢。

No. 1

When the House of Chin settled here,
A new capital did appear.
The terrain's good for kings on earth;
The mountains like tigers pry forth.
Gold Hill is grandiose in vain;
The Heaven Trench does calm remain.
While drunk, back home I ply my oar;
The merry Wu tune rings to soar.

* the House of Chin: In the Western Chin dynasty, there burst the most severe strife in the royal house which lasted sixteen years and involved more than eight sovereigns.
* Gold Hill: referring to Nanking, one of the most well-known ancient cities in China, a strategic fort as a gateway to the sea, which has been the capital of Wu, Chin, and many other states or kingdoms, such as the six empires called Six Dynasties and has

flourished immensely with increasing trade and travel.
* the Heaven Trench: referring to the Yangtze River that safeguards Gold Hill like a trench from Heaven.
* Wu: the area south of the Yangtze River, a place that belonged to the State of Wu in the Spring and Autumn period and the Kingdom of Wu in the Three Kingdoms period.

其 二

地拥金陵势，
城回江水流。
当时百万户，
夹道起朱楼。
亡国生春草，
王宫没古丘。
空馀后湖月，
波上对瀛洲。

No. 2

The terrain from above looks down;
The river flows around the town.
Those rich families brightly gilt
Along high ways their mansions built.
The paradise lost teems with grass;
The courts are sunk in dirt, alas.
The moon o'er the lake hangs in vain;
Fairyland shades waves of the main.

* the moon: the planet of the earth, which appears at night and gives off shining silvery light. The wax and wane of the moon symbolizes the vicissitudes of life or of the world.
* Fairyland: name of a shoal in this poem, regarded as a Chinese elysium.

其 三

六代兴亡国，
三杯为尔歌。
苑方秦地少，
山似洛阳多。
古殿吴花草，
深宫晋绮罗。
并随人事灭，
东逝与沧波。

No. 3

The six dynasties are all gone;
Three cups drunk, I'll sing to go on.
This place has fewer parks than West Land;
Than in Loshine more hills here stand.
In the broad hall Wu's blooms were laid;
In the palace kept was Chin's brocade.
All with the dynasties have died;
But the river swells up to tide.

* the six dynasties: referring to six regimes that adopted Gold Hill as their capital.
* West Land: referring to the land west of Case Dale, which is mainly Ch'in's land.
* Loshine: Loyang if transliterated, the second largest city, the eastern capital in the T'ang dynasty.
* Wu: the area south of Gold Hill.
* Chin: referring to the Kingdom of Chin including Western Chin and the Eastern Chin.

秋夜板桥浦泛月独酌怀谢朓

天上何所有？
迢迢白玉绳。
斜低建章阙，
耿耿对金陵。
汉水旧如练，
霜江夜清澄。
长川泻落月，
洲渚晓寒凝。
独酌板桥浦，
古人谁可徵？
玄晖难再得，
洒酒气填膺。

Drinking and Missing T'iao Hsieh in Slab Bridge Shore on an Autumn Night

What can we see in the blue sky?
Jade Rope Stars far away and high.
To Chapter Palace it'd come near;
At Gold Hill it looks with a leer.
The water shimmers like cloth white;
The river's dyed with frost at night.
The Yangtze pours moonbeams there lost;
The shoal is frozen with hoarfrost.
On the slab bridge I drink my wine;
Of ancients who've come here to dine?

> Poets like T'iao Hsieh I cannot find;
> I splash wine to my troubled mind.

* Slab Bridge Shore: 20 kilometers from Gold Hill, which is today's Nanking, Chiangsu Province.
* Jade Rope Stars: a constellation in general.
* Chapter Palace: a palace built by Emperor Martial of Han in 104 B.C., with a suspension passage to Non-end Palace in the other part of the capital. This palace was actually a group of different complexes with walls.
* The Yangtze: the Yangtze River, the longest river in China.
* Gold Hill: referring to today's Nanking, one of the most well-known ancient capitals in China.
* T'iao Hsieh: T'iao Hsieh (A.D. 464 – A.D. 499), an outstanding highborn landscape poet.

过彭蠡湖

谢公入彭蠡，
因此游松门。
余方窥石镜，
兼得穷江源。
前赏迹可见，
后来道空存。
而欲继风雅，
岂惟清心魂。
云海方助兴，
波涛何足论？
青嶂忆遥月，
绿萝愁鸣猿。
水碧或可采，
金膏秘莫言。
余将振衣去，
羽化出嚣烦。

A Visit to P'oshine Lake

Lord Glee once came to P'oshine Lake;
To Mt. Pinegate he did tours make.
Stone Mirror I would peer into
And row away on ripples blue.
The seniors past were high, much higher;
Where can I true knowledge acquire?
I'll learn the lord's pursuits refined,

Not just to entertain my mind.
The clouded ocean will soon surge;
Will breakers all dirt and filth purge?
The laurels shade Luna's faint shine;
The creepers hear the monkeys' whine.
For emerald, rocks may be mined;
Where can we a golden knack find?
To learn the Word I'll go away,
And rise out of the world I may.

* P'oshine Lake: the largest freshwater lake of China, in the north of Chianghsi and south of the Long River.
* Lord Glee: the court title of Lingyün Hsieh (A.D. 385 – A.D. 433), a highborn poet, idyllist, Buddhist and traveler, famous for landscape poems.
* Mt. Pinegate: 100 kilometers from Yüchang, surrounded by a river and lush with pine trees.
* Stone Mirror: there is stone by Kungt'ing Lake, round and smooth like a mirror.
* laurel: an evergreen shrub with aromatic, lance-shaped leaves, yellowish flowers, and succulent, cherry-like fruit, a symbol of glory usually in the form of a crown or wreath of laurel to indicate honor or high merit, especially when one had passed Grand Test, i.e. Civil Service Examinations for selecting government officials, in ancient China. In Chinese mythology, there is a colossal laurel tree on the moon, and it would never fall even though Kang Wu, a banished immortal, has kept cutting it.
* Luna: the moon, an important image of solitude or altitude in Chinese culture.

入彭蠡，经松门观石镜，缅怀谢康乐，题诗书游览之志

谢公之彭蠡，
因此游松门。
余方窥石镜，
兼得穷江源。
将欲继风雅，
岂徒清心魂。
前赏逾所见，
后来道空存。
况属临泛美，
而无洲渚喧。
漾水向东去，
漳流直南奔。
空濛三川夕，
回合千里昏。
青桂隐遥月，
绿枫鸣愁猿。
水碧或可采，
金精秘莫论。
吾将学仙去，
冀与琴高言。

Looking into Stone Mirror on Mt. Pinegate on My Way to P'oshine, Reminiscing Lord Glee and Writing a Verse to Express My Will

Once Lord Glee came to P'oshine Lake;
To Mt. Pinegate he did tours make.
Stone Mirror I would look into
And row afar on ripples blue.
I'll learn Lord Glee's pursuits refined,
Not just to entertain my mind.
The seniors past were high, much higher;
Where can I true knowledge acquire?
A flood season will soon begin,
There is no noise, uproar or din.
The Yang River to the east flows;
The Chang River to the south goes.
The two rivers meet the lake here;
The water does expand, so blear.
The laurels shade the moon's faint shine;
The maples hear the monkeys' whine.
For emerald, rocks may be mined;
Where can we a golden knack find?
To learn the Word I will depart
And talk with a saint heart to heart.

* Mt. Pinegate: 100 kilometers from Yüchang, surrounded by a river and lush with pine trees.

* Lord Glee: the court title of Lingyün Hsieh (A.D. 385 - A.D. 433), a highborn poet,

Buddhist and traveler, famous for landscape poems.
* P'oshine Lake: the largest freshwater lake of China in present-day Chianghsi Province and the Long River.
* the Yang River: an ancient river located at the upper stretch of the Han.
* the Chang River: a river in today's Hupei Province.
* maple: any of a large genus (*Acer*) of deciduous trees of the north temperate zone, with opposite leaves that turn red in autumn and a fruit of two joined samaras, a symbol of cordial love and good luck because of its bright fiery color.
* the Word: referring to Tao if transliterated, the most significant and profoundest concept in Chinese philosophy, identifiable with the Word or the Logos in western philosophy, as there is an enormous amount of common ground in the two cosmologies and the doctrines concerning the most fundamental matters such as "the Word is the One" and "God is the One", and the personalization of Being, the progenitor of finite spirits, which are subordinate kinds of Being or merely appearances of the Divine, the One.

庐江主人妇

孔雀东飞何处栖，
庐江小吏仲卿妻。
为客裁缝君自见，
城乌独宿夜空啼。

A Wife in Lodgeriver

The peacock flies east for a better life;
In Lodgeriver, the Clerk Ching has a wife.
She darns clothes for passengers who pass by;
In the trees by the wall, crows at night cry.

* Lodgeriver: referring to present-day Ch'ienshan County, Anhui Province.
* peacock: the male of a gallinaceous crested bird (genus *Pavo*), which has the tail coverts enormously elongated, erectile, and marked with ocelli or eyelike spots and the neck and breast of an irridescent greenish blue.
* the Clerk Ching: referring to Chungch'ing Chiao, a figure in a verse in the late Eastern Han dynasty. In the verse, he and his wife both committed suicide under the oppression of their families.
* crow: an omnivorous, raucous, oscine bird of the genus *Corvus*, with glossy black plumage. It is regarded as an ominous bird, a metaphor for death because it is a scavenger, feeding on carrion. It is a common image in Chinese literature, which can be found in *The Book of Songs* compiled 2500 years ago: "Crows are all black, it's said, / So as foxes are red."

陪宋中丞武昌夜饮怀古

清景南楼夜，
风流在武昌。
庾公爱秋月，
乘兴坐胡床。
龙笛吟寒水，
天河落晓霜。
我心还不浅，
怀古醉余觞。

Drinking at Night with Magistrate Sung to Reminisce the Past in Mightboom

How serene South Tower is at night!
Here in Mightboom are talents bright.
You, like Lord Yü, love moonlit cool,
With leisure sitting on the stool.
There floats downstream a cold flute lay
While frost falls from the Milky Way.
In high spirits, I am still up;
For those saints past, let's drain our cup.

* Mightboom: Wuch'ang if transliterated, an important county in history, now the central part of the tripartite unity of Wuhan, Hupei Province.
* Lord Yü: referring to Liang Yü (A.D. 289 – A.D. 340), renowned scholar in the Eastern Chin dynasty.
* stool: formerly called Hun stool, an armless and backless collapsible seat intended for

one person, introduced to China in the Han dynasty.
* the Milky Way: a luminous band circling the heavens composed of stars and nebulae; the Galaxy.

望鹦鹉洲怀祢衡

魏帝营八极，
蚁观一祢衡。
黄祖斗筲人，
杀之受恶名。
吴江赋鹦鹉，
落笔超群英。
锵锵振金玉，
句句欲飞鸣。
鸷鹗啄孤凤，
千春伤我情。
五岳起方寸，
隐然讵可平。
才高竟何施，
寡识冒天刑。
至今芳洲上，
兰蕙不忍生。

Missing Scale Mi While Gazing at Parrot Shoal

Lord Way ruled the world and ruled all;
To him Scale was an ant so small.
Huang was so menial, a base one;
He killed Scale, ill-famed, ill-done.
Scale at the Wu did *Parrot* write,
Outshining so many poets bright.

Each and every word seams to ring;
Each and every line seems to sing.
The phoenix was by a hawk killed;
With the age-old sadness I'm filled.
The five mountains rise in my chest;
How can I make the surge at rest?
His talent not put to full play,
Short-sighted, he died the cruel way.
Today there on the fragrant shoal,
No orchids grow, not e'en a soul.

* Scale Mi: referring to Heng Mi (A.D. 173 – A.D. 198) if transliterated, an upright man in the Three Kingdoms period. When Mi was banished to Riversummer, the prefect's son, prefect of another prefecture, gave him a parrot and required him to write a verse about it. Mi finished *Ode to the Parrot* a long poem of about seven hundred words without stop, comparing the parrot to himself.
* Parrot Shoal: a shoal located in today's Wuhan, Hupei Province.
* Lord Way: referring to Ts'ao Ts'ao (A.D. 155 – A.D. 220), a super lord in the Three Kingdoms period, the founder of Way (A.D. 213 – A.D. 266), the most powerful of the three kingdoms in that period.
* Huang: Referring to Chu Huang (? – A.D. 208), who had Scale Mi killed when infuriated by the latter's harsh words.
* the Wu: referring to the Wu River, a tributary of the Yangtze River.
* orchid: any of a widely distributed family of terrestrial or epiphytic monocotyledonous plants having thickened bulbous roots and often very showy distinctive flowers, one of the four most important floral images in Chinese literature, which are wintersweet, orchid, bamboo and chrysanthemum.

宿 巫 山 下

昨夜巫山下，
猿声梦里长。
桃花飞绿水，
三月下瞿塘。
雨色风吹去，
南行拂楚王。
高丘怀宋玉，
访古一沾裳。

Putting Up for the Night Below Mt. Witch

Below Mt. Witch I spent the night;
The monkeys shrieked long in my dream.
O'er blue water, March blooms in flight,
I'm in Big Pond, rowing downstream.
The wind does the rain to south blow
To wet the clothes on King of Ch'u.
I miss Jade Sung on the mound here,
My eyes so warming, full of tear.

* Mt. Witch: a mythical and religious mountain, which was thought to be a range of mountains in Shanhsi. As the witchcraft culture spread south, many mountains were named after Mt. Witch, for example, the one in the Three Gorges area of the Long River.
* Big Pond: one of the three gorges of the Long River.
* King of Ch'u: probably referring to King Huai of Ch'u.

* Jade Sung: Jade Sung (cir. 298 B.C.- cir. 222 B.C.), one of the four most handsome men in ancient China, a student of Yüan Ch'ü's, and a famous poet in the Warring States period. He once served as an official for King Hsiang of Ch'u.

金陵白杨十字巷

白杨十字巷，
北夹湖沟道。
不见吴时人，
空生唐年草。
天地有反覆，
宫城尽倾倒。
六帝馀古丘，
樵苏泣遗老。

White Poplar Crossroads Lane in Gold Hill

There is White Poplar Crossroads Lane,
North of it is the flood-fight drain.
The Wu folks from here are all gone;
The grass of T'ang in vain scrawls on.
Heaven and earth turn, time elapsed;
The palaces have all collapsed.
The six dynasties gone, now old clay,
The folks left are woodsmen today.

* White Poplar Crossroads Lane: name of a road, also known as White Poplar Road, 6 kilometers from Up One County, near present-day Nanking, Chiangsu Province.
* Gold Hill: referring to Nanking, one of the most well-known ancient capitals in China.
* the Wu folks: the folks south of the Yangtze River, in the sphere of Wu culture.
* T'ang: the T'ang Empire (A.D. 618 – A.D. 907), a great prosperous empire after the Sui dynasty, one of the best empires in Chinese history. The T'ang dynasty was the

golden age of Chinese Poetry—In the number of poems and variety of poetic forms, the beauty of imagery and broadness of themes, T'ang Poetry surpasses all that had preceded it.

* the Six Dynasties: the six different regimes of Wu, Chin, Sung, Ch'i, Liang, and Ch'en that had Gold Hill as their capital are regarded as six dynasties in Chinese history.

谢 公 亭

谢亭离别处，
风景每生愁。
客散青天月，
山空碧水流。
池花春映日，
窗竹夜鸣秋。
今古一相接，
长歌怀旧游。

Lord Glee's Kiosk

Lord Glee's Kiosk's a place to say bye;
Whene'er I see the scene, I sigh.
Friends parting, the moon faintly glows;
The hills void, the lonely rill flows.
The vernal lilies bloom or blight;
The autumn bamboo soughs at night.
Past or present, real friends are few;
A long song I sing but for you.

* Lord Glee's Kiosk: a stone pavilion near Mt. West Pagoda in E'erfair (Yungkia) in today's Wenchow, Chechiang Province. Lord Glee, i.e., Lingyün Hsieh (A.D. 385 - A.D. 433), a highborn poet and Buddhist, was once the prefect of E'erfair, so the kiosk was named after him in memory of him, and he was remembered as a mountain climber, who invented special mountain shoes.
* the moon: the celestial body that revolves around the earth from west to east as a satellite, which appears at night and gives off shining silvery light and the roundedness

of which denotes happy reunion.
* lily: any of a large genus (*Lilium*) of perennial plants of the lily family, grown from a bulb, and having typically trumpet-shaped flowers, white or colored.

纪南陵题五松山

圣达有去就，
潜光愚其德。
鱼与龙同池，
龙去鱼不测。
当时板筑辈，
岂知傅说情。
一朝和殷羹，
光气为列星。
伊尹生空桑，
捐庖佐皇极。
桐宫放太甲，
摄政无愧色。
三年帝道明，
委质终辅翼。
旷哉至人心，
万古可为则。
时命或大缪，
仲尼将奈何？
鸾凤忽覆巢，
麒麟不来过。
龟山蔽鲁国，
有斧且无柯。
归来归去来，
宵济越洪波。

Writing an Inscription on Mt. Five Pines in Southridge

Saints appear here or go afar;
Free of care or detached they are.
Fish and dragons the same pool share;
When dragons fly, no fish know e'er.
The slaves who with Fu hard days passed
Ne'er knew he rose to power so fast.
When by King Wuting he was praised,
He shone with the stars, so up raised.
Yin was born in a mulberry wood,
Raised by Cook, help the king he could.
He put bad Crown Prince in a cell;
A regent, he was doing well.
In three years Crown Prince was king made;
Yin still helped him, as his good aide.
This story's been to all passed on;
Yin's an all-time sage, a good one.
Each person may have his great rue;
With this what could Confucius do?
Phoenixes may o'erturn their nest;
Unicorns may not come, depressed.
Mt. Turtle can the Lu State shade;
An axe may have no handle made.
I'll go there, go there to abide,
And wait in hiding for the tide.

* Mt. Five Pines: located in present-day Copperridge (T'ungling), Anhui Province, so named because there grew five pines on the very top. According to *Geographical Wonders* compiled in the Southern Sung dynasty, "The mountain boasted old pines, five in one, a pentad, reaching high to the sky with scale-like bark on the trunk."

* Southridge: Southridge County in today's Anhui Province, a gateway to Two Mountains and One Lake (Mt. Yellow, Mt. Nine Flowers, and Great Peace Lake), established as a county in A.D. 525 by Emperor Martial of Liang (A.D. 464 - A.D. 549) in the Southern Dynasties period.
* Fu: referring to Yüeh Fu (Master Joy), a noble minister of high reputation in the Shang dynasty.
* King Wuting: King Wuting (? - 1192 B.C.), one of the most capable kings of Shang. Under his governance, Shang prospered in all aspects.
* Yin: referring to Yin Ee (1649 B.C.- 1550 B.C.), a statesman, thinker, founding commander of Shang, and one of the founders of Wordism.
* mulberry: the edible, berry-like fruit of a tree (genus *Morus*) whose leaves are valued for silkworm culture, and the tree itself.
* Confucius: Confucius (551 B.C. - 479 B.C.), a renowned thinker, educator and statesman in the Spring and Autumn period, born in the State of Lu, who was the founder of Confucianism, and has exerted profound influence on Chinese culture.
* phoenix: a legendary bird, the king of all birds, a symbol of good luck and nobility.
* unicorn: a fabulous deer-like animal with one horn, a symbol of saintliness and divinity in Chinese culture. Confucius lamented the death of a unicorn captured and hence stopped compiling *The Spring and Autumn Annals* and died before long.
* Mt. Turtle: a mountain in the State of Lu. Confucius failed in admonishing his lord and made a verse at Mt. Turtle.
* the Lu State: the State of Lu, the state enfeoffed to Prince of Chough, inherited by his son Firstling Bird, exterminated by Ch'u in 256 B.C.

夜泊牛渚怀古

牛渚西江夜，
青天无片云。
登舟望秋月，
空忆谢将军。
余亦能高咏，
斯人不可闻。
明朝挂帆席，
枫叶落纷纷。

One Night on Mt. Ox Shoal

Ox Shoal at night, the West flows by,
Not a single cloud in the sky.
I step aboard to view the moon,
And seem to hear Marshal Hsieh's croon.
Sing out in a loud voice I can,
But not in response to this man.
I'll set my sail tomorrow morn,
With maple leaves fluttering down.

* Mt. Ox Shoal: a mountain 17.5 kilometers from present-day Tangt'u, Anhui Province.
* the moon: the planet of the earth, which appears at night and gives off shining silvery light. As it is alone, it is assigned a meaning of solitude or a wish for a happy reunion.
* Marshal Hsieh: referring to Shang Hsieh (A.D. 308 – A.D. 357), General An Hsieh's cousin, a renowned commander in the Eastern Chin dynasty.
* maple: any of a large genus (*Acer*) of deciduous trees of the north temperate zone, with opposite leaves that turn red in autumn and a fruit of two joined samaras, a symbol of cordial love and good luck because of its bright fiery color.

姑 孰 溪

爱此溪水闲，
乘流兴无极。
漾楫怕鸥惊，
垂竿待鱼食。
波翻晓霞影，
岸叠春山色。
何处浣纱人？
红颜未相识。

The Kushu Stream

I love this stream, a peaceful stream;
I row and row with fun extreme.
Shoo, gulls! I stop my oar and wait;
I drop the fishing rod with bait.
The waves stir clouds dropped to the blue;
The banks are piled with mountain hue.
Who's the maid washing yarn, who?
Why, such a beauty I don't know!

* the Kushu Stream: a stream in today's Tangt'u, Anhui Province. As is recorded in Journal on *My Trip to Shu* by Yu Lu (A.D. 1125 – A.D. 1210), a Southern Sung poet, "The stream is blue, and clear like a mirror, and minnows passing or coming can be counted."
* gull: seagull, a kind of sea bird, any gull or large tern, a symbol of clean integrity. The seagulls in the Wordist book *Sir Line* (Liehtzu) are particularly sensitive to impurity of motive and will make friends only with the completely guileless and disinterested.

丹　阳　湖

湖与元气连，
风波浩难止。
天外贾客归，
云间片帆起。
龟游莲叶上，
鸟宿芦花里。
少女棹轻舟，
歌声逐流水。

Lake Redshine

The lake links with the blue on high;
The waves do rush on without stop.
The merchant ship comes out of the sky;
The sail greets me with clouds atop.
A turtle boards a lotus leaf;
The birds are nestled on the reeds.
The maiden rows the little skiff;
There flows a song that the flow leads.

* Lake Redshine: a lake 37.5 kilometers from Tangt'u, at the lower stretch of the Yangtze River.
* skiff: a light rowboat for fishing or lotus-picking and so on; formerly a sailing vessel.

谢 公 宅

青山日将暝，
寂寞谢公宅。
竹里无人声，
池中虚月白。
荒庭衰草遍，
废井苍苔积。
唯有清风闲，
时时起泉石。

Lord Glee's House

The night's about, the green hill sees;
So calm is the house of Lord Glee's.
No human noise in the bamboo;
The moon white in the pool so blue.
In the abandoned yard grass dries;
To the deserted well moss pries.
The wind blows, so free, all alone,
As sighs and sighs to the spring stone.

* Lord Glee: Lingyün Hsieh (A.D. 385 – A.D. 433), a highborn poet, Buddhist, idyllist and traveler, famous for landscape poems, inherited the title Lord Glee from his grandfather, Hsuan Hsieh (A.D. 343 – A.D. 388), a famous general of Eastern Chin.
* bamboo: a tall, tree-like or shrubby grass in tropical and semi-tropical regions, a symbol of integrity and altitude, one of the four most important images in Chinese literature, which are wintersweet, orchid, bamboo and chrysanthemum.
* the moon: the celestial body that revolves around the earth from west to east as a

satellite, which is an image of purity and solitude in Chinese culture.
* moss: a tiny, delicate green bryophytic plant growing on damp decaying wood, wet ground, humid rocks or trees, producing capsules which open by an operculum and contain spores. Under a poet's writing brush, it may arouse a poetic feeling or imagination.

凌歇台

旷望登古台，
台高极人目。
叠嶂列远空，
杂花间平陆。
闲云入窗牖，
野翠生松竹。
欲览碑上文，
苔侵岂堪读？

Rising Mound

To gaze afar I climb the mound;
The mound high, I could see around.
The hills are layered in the sky;
The plain sees trees and blossoms vie.
Free clouds come to approach my door;
Pines and bamboos grow on the moor.
The words on the stele I'd look at;
With much moss, how could I do that?

---

* Rising Mound: a summer resort built on Mt. Yellow by Chun Liu (A.D. 430 – A.D. 464), Emperor Pious Might of Sung (A.D. 363 – A.D. 422), the fifth emperor of Sung in the Southern and Northern Dynasties.
* pine: any of a genus (*Pinus*) of evergreen trees of the pine family, a cone-bearing tree having bundles of two to five needle-shaped leaves growing in clusters, an important image in Chinese literature, a symbol of rectitude, longevity and so on.
* bamboo: a tall, tree-like or shrubby grass in tropical and semi-tropical regions, a

symbol of integrity fortitude and altitude. A Ching poet speaks of its character in a poem *Bamboo Rooted in the Rock*: "You bite the green hill and ne'er rest. / Roots in the broken crag, you grow, / And stand erect although hard pressed. / East, west, south, north, let the wind blow."

* moor: a tract of open, rolling wetland, usually covered with heather and often marshy or peaty. Natural places like moors, glades, coves, hills, rivers, mounts and seas, and so on often allude to reclusion in Chinese culture.
* moss: a delicate bryophytic plant growing on damp decaying wood, wet ground, humid rocks or trees, producing capsules which open by an operculum and contain spores. Under a poet's writing brush, it may arouse a poetic feeling or imagination.

桓 公 井

桓公名已古，
废井曾未竭。
石甃冷苍苔，
寒泉湛孤月。
秋来桐暂落，
春至桃还发。
路远人罕窥，
谁能见清澈？

Lord Pillar's Well

Long ago the well-digger died;
The well deserted has ne'er dried.
The brick wall is with cold moss grown;
The cool spring shows a disc of moon.
In autumn phoenix leaves are blast;
In springtime peach blossoms blow fast.
Few passengers have come in here;
Who can e'er see the well so clear?

* Lord Pillar: referring to Wen Huan (A.D. 312 – A.D. 373), a military strategist and statesman of Eastern Chin.
* Lord Pillar's Well: dug by Commander Wen Huan (A.D. 312 – A.D. 373) on Mt. White Ramie, 2.5 kilometers from present-day Tangt'u, Anhui Province.
* peach: any tree of the genus *Prunus Percica*, blooming brilliantly and bearing fruit, a fleshy, juicy, edible drupe, considered sacred in China, a symbol of romance, prosperity and longevity.

慈姥竹

野竹攒石生，
含烟映江岛。
翠色落波深，
虚声带寒早。
龙吟曾未听，
凤曲吹应好。
不学蒲柳凋，
贞心常自保。

Loving Granny's Bamboo

From the rubble wild bamboo grows;
O'er the island straying mist flows.
The emerald dyes the waves throughout;
The silent sounds bring chills about.
I have ne'er heard a dragon sing;
The phoenix flute should better ring.
Don't learn from cattail that lies waste;
One should remain loyal and chaste.

* Loving Granny: referring to Mt. Granny, a mountain in today's Tangt'u, Anhui Province.
* bamboo: a tall, tree-like or shrubby grass in tropical and semi-tropical regions, a symbol of integrity fortitude and altitude. A Ching poet speaks of its character in a poem *Bamboo Rooted in the Rock*: "You bite the green hill and ne'er rest. / Roots in the broken crag, you grow, / And stand erect although hard pressed. / East, west, south, north, let the wind blow."

* dragon: a fabulous serpent-like giant winged animal that can change its girth and length, a symbol of benevolence and sovereignty in Chinese culture.
* the phoenix flute: the flute that sounds like a phoenix sings; a praise of a flute tune.
* cattail: a perennial acquatic plant (genus *Typha*), with long leaves, flowers in cylindrical terminal spikes, and downy fruit.

望 夫 山

颙望临碧空,
怨情感离别。
江草不知愁,
岩花但争发。
云山万重隔,
音信千里绝。
春去秋复来,
相思几时歇?

Mt. O Come Hubby

I look up and into the sky;
When starting off, with rue I sigh.
The river grass never knows woe;
The blossoms on rocks vie to blow.
My man beyond the hills away;
There is no news from him, o nay.
Spring goes and autumn comes again,
When can I rest with no more pain?

* Mt. O Come Hubby: a mountain 28.5 kilometers from Tangt'u. A man went to Ch'u and did not come back home in a few years, and his wife climbed onto the mountain to look where her husband might be and turned into a stone, hence the name of the mountain. More than one hill in China has taken this name because of a similar case of a wife who climbed the height to watch for the return of her husband.

牛 渚 矶

绝壁临巨川,
连峰势相向。
乱石流洑间,
回波自成浪。
但惊群木秀,
莫测精灵状。
更听猿夜啼,
忧心醉江上。

Ox Shoal Boulder

The cliffs see the giant river race;
The peaks do tower up face to face.
The boulder to the whirlpool raves;
The eddies backward throw up waves.
At the verdant plants I wonder;
I dare not guess the devils under.
The monkeys at night sadly scream;
I feel sad, as if drunk downstream.

* Ox Shoal Boulder: a protrusion of rock under Mt. Ox Shoal, a mountain in present-day Anhui Province.
* monkey: any of a group of primates usually having a flat, hairless face, elongate limbs, hands and feet adapted for grasping, and a highly developed nervous system, including marmosets, baboons, and macaques, but not the anthropoid apes, though monkeys and apes are used alternatively in Chinese, also used as a metaphor for somebody who is mischievous and shrewdly calculating.

灵 墟 山

丁令辞世人，
拂衣向仙路。
伏炼九丹成，
方随五云去。
松萝蔽幽洞，
桃杏深隐处。
不知曾化鹤，
辽海归几度？

Mt. Soul's Wasteland

Jingle to the world adieu bade;
To be a saint, his clothes he threw.
When elixir was by him made,
He followed the hued clouds to go.
The pine trailers o'er the cave spread;
In the deep wood he may abide.
He has become a crane instead;
How oft comes he to the seaside?

* Jingle: referring to Lingwei Ting if transliterated, a Wordist immortal.
* elixir: a kind of cure-all concocted from refined cinnabar by Wordist alchemists.
* hued clouds: a sign of auspiciousness.
* crane: one of a family of large, long-necked, long-legged, heronlike birds allied to the rails, a symbol of integrity and longevity in Chinese culture, only second to the phoenix in cultural importance.

天　门　山

迥出江上山，
双峰自相对。
岸映松色寒，
石分浪花碎。
参差远天际，
缥缈晴霞外。
落日舟去遥，
回首沉青霭。

Mt. Skygate

Far off the river looms the hill;
The two peaks tower up face to face.
The banks reflect the pines so chill;
The rock break the blue waves apace.
The sky sees hills roll high and low,
Ethereal beyond the cloud rays.
Towards the setting sun I row;
Turning back, I feel sunk in haze.

* Mt. Skygate: mountains located on the two banks of the Yangtze River southwest of Tangt'u, one mountain on the northern bank, and the other on the southern. The two mountains stand opposite like a gate, hence the name.
* pine: any of a genus (*Pinus*) of evergreen trees of the pine family, a cone-bearing tree having bundles of two to five needle-shaped leaves growing in clusters, an important image in Chinese literature, a symbol of rectitude, longevity and so on.

古近体诗四十七首
Old-new Rhythmic Poetry, 47 Poems

与元丹丘方城寺谈玄作

茫茫大梦中,
惟我独先觉。
腾转风火来,
假合作容貌。
灭除昏疑尽,
领略入精要。
澄虑观此身,
因得通寂照。
郎悟前后际,
始知金仙妙。
幸逢禅居人,
酌玉坐相召。
彼我俱若丧,
云山岂殊调。
清风生虚空,
明月见谈笑。
怡然青莲宫,
永愿恣游眺。

Talking about Sutra with Redknoll Yüan in Squareton Temple

Haze, haze, in their dream they all sleep;
But I come to the realization.
Wind and fire turn and turn, and sweep;
There now comes the composition.

With this, you get rid of your doubt,
And come to know what's finely true.
Doubtless, you turn and look about,
And find the void is lightened through.
You are aware what's Fore and Then,
And recognize Buddha divine.
I meet you here practising Zen,
And we invite each oth'r to wine.
We both feel lost, no means employed;
The clouds and mountains merge as one.
A breeze blows now into the void;
The moon sees us laugh—all is fun.
We'd sit in Green Lotus at ease
Or tour sights and heights as we please.

* sutra: a formulated doctrine, often so short as to be unintelligible without a key; literally a rule or a precept. In Buddhism, it is an extended writing usually in verse, and often in dialogue form, embodying important religious and philosophical propositions, sometimes directly, sometimes in highly allegorical or metaphorical language. The best example is a dialogue between two monks, Hsiu Shen and Neng Hui. The former's verse is like this: "The body is a Bodhi tree; / The mind's like a mirror stand bright. / Make it clean, as oft as can be, / In case dust should on it alight." And Neng Hui replied, bettering the former: "There's nothing like a Bodhi tree, / Nor such things as a mirror stand. / There is nothing that you can see. / Where can dust find a place to land?"
* Redknoll Yüan: a Wordist and an important friend of Pai Li's. Pai Li met him at the age of twenty and once lived in seclusion with him on Mt. Tower.
* Squareton Temple: unidentified.
* Zen: a kind of performance of quietude in a form of meditation or contemplation. When Sanskrit jana was introduced to China, it was translated as Zan or Zen for this kind of practice. In the T'ang dynasty, Zen had become very influential among the intellectuals, many of whom were associated with Zen monks and spent time in Zen monasteries.
* Green Lotus: a metaphor for a Buddhist temple; Pai Li's Buddhist name.

寻高凤石门山中元丹丘

寻幽无前期,
乘兴不觉远。
苍崖渺难涉,
白日忽欲晚。
未穷三四山,
已历千万转。
寂寂闻猿愁,
行行见云收。
高松来好月,
空谷宜清秋。
溪深古雪在,
石断寒泉流。
峰峦秀中天,
登眺不可尽。
丹丘遥相呼,
顾我忽而哂。
遂造穷谷间,
始知静者闲。
留欢达永夜,
清晓方言还。

Visiting Redknoll Yüan in Hiphoenix's Mt. Stonegate

No appointment, not agreed on,
I tour myself, with enough fun.

The crag so high is hard to climb;
It's late—fast elapses the time.
Not more peaks I've scaled, three or four;
I've turned and turned, now back, now fore.
Calm, so calm, only monkeys cry;
Flown, off flown, clouds go off the sky.
The tall pines see the crescent shine;
The void vale blows to autumn fine.
The valleys contain age-old snow;
The rock worn lets out a spring flow.
The peaks tower up to scrape the sky;
All wonders, far off or nearby.
Redknoll, you greet me from afar;
With a laugh, how happy you are!
Only when I've toured all the dales
Do I know calm or void prevails.
I play and linger here all night,
And go back in the dawning light.

* Redknoll Yüan: a Wordist adept and an important friend of Pai Li's. With their twenty-four years' friendship and correspondence, Rendknoll exerted great influence on Pai Li, who wrote 14 poems dedicated to the former.
* Mt. Stonegate: a Buddhist attraction probably in today's Huaijou, an area of Peking.
* Hiphoenix: a recluse who once taught in the hills of West T'ang.

安州般若寺水阁纳凉，喜遇薛员外乂

翛然金园赏，
远近含晴光。
楼台成海气，
草木皆天香。
忽逢青云士，
共解丹霞裳。
水退池上热，
风生松下凉。
吞讨破万象，
搴窥临众芳。
而我遗有漏，
与君用无方。
心垢都已灭，
永言题禅房。

Enjoying the Cool in Prajna Temple in Peaceton, Where I Meet Worth Hsüeh, a Ministry Councillor

In Gold Park I have had much fun,
Enjoying warm light from the sun.
The tower's like mist over the brine,
The grass imbued with balm divine.
A hermit I now bump into;
He doffs his robe with clouded hue.
Some heat arises from the pool,

And the pines give rise to some cool.
Between breaths you have all with you;
The blooms you want to stroke or view.
My defects I'd throw to the ground,
So we could travel without bound.
Of dirt my heart is cleansed, and then
I'll write an inscription for Zen.

* Prajna Temple: a Buddhist temple in Peaceton, i.e. today's Anlu County, Hupei Province.
* Peaceton: the Prefecture of Peaceton, in present-day Anlu County, Hupei Province.
* Zen: a kind of performance of quietude in a form of meditation or contemplation. When the Sanskrit word jana was introduced to China, it was translated as Zan or Zen for this kind of practice. In the T'ang dynasty, Zen had become very influential among the intellectuals, many of whom were associated with Zen monks and spent time in Zen monasteries.

鲁中都东楼醉起作

昨日东楼醉，
还应倒接䍦。
阿谁扶上马，
不省下楼时。

Written on East Tower When Drunk in Midtown of Lu

East Tower saw me drunk yesterday;
By the hedge I fell and there lay.
Helped to ride my horse unawares!
Not yet sober, coming downstairs!

* Midtown: Midtown County in the T'ang dynasty, in today's Shantung Province.
* horse: a large herbivorous solid-hoofed quadruped (*Equus caballus*) with a coarse mane and tail, of various strains: Ferghana, Mongolian, Kazaks, Hequ, Karasahr and so on, and of various colors: black, white, yellow, brown, dappled and so on, commonly in the domesticated state, employed as a beast of draught and burden and especially for riding upon.

对酒醉题屈突明府厅

陶令八十日，
长歌归去来。
故人建昌宰，
借问几时回？
风落吴江雪，
纷纷入酒杯。
山翁今已醉，
舞袖为君开。

Writing an Inscription for Magistrate Ch'ut'u's Hall When Drunk

After eighty days to a day,
T'ao sang: I'll go home, go away.
Magistrate of Buildboom, my friend,
When will you go home, back there wend?
The southern snow a wind swirls up,
While snowflakes fall into the cup.
Now friend, you are drunk, in a trance
Let me wave my sleeves for your dance.

* T'ao: referring to Poolbright T'ao (A.D. 352 – A.D. 427), an official, verse writer, poet, and litterateur in the Chin dynasty, and the founder of Chinese idyllism. Poolbright was once the magistrate of P'engtse, and he resigned from his official post four times in order to live in seclusion.
* Buildboom: referring to Chiench'ang, a county in the T'ang dynasty.

月下独酌四首

Drinking Alone Under the Moon, Four Poems

其 一

花间一壶酒，
独酌无相亲。
举杯邀明月，
对影成三人。
月既不解饮，
影徒随我身。
暂伴月将影，
行乐须及春。
我歌月徘徊，
我舞影零乱。
醒时同交欢，
醉后各分散。
永结无情游，
相期邈云汉。

No. 1

Amid the blooms, a pot of wine,
I drink alone with no friends mine.
Cup raised, the moon I now invite,
With my shadow, three for the night.
To drink my wine the moon's not fain;
My shadow follows me in vain.

Let them stay with me for a time;
I must enjoy life while in prime.
My singing does the moon entrance;
My shadow's disturbed as I dance.
While I'm sober, haply they stay;
Once I'm drunk, fast they go away.
Cool friendship we will keep for e'er
And meet in the Milky Way there.

* the moon: the planet of the earth, which appears at night and gives off shining silvery light, an image of purity and solitude, and a representation of feminity as a source of Shade.
* the Milky Way: known as the Silver River in Chinese culture; a luminous band circling the heavens composed of stars and nebulae; the Galaxy.

其 二

天若不爱酒，
酒星不在天。
地若不爱酒，
地应无酒泉。
天地既爱酒，
爱酒不愧天。
已闻清比圣，
复道浊如贤。
贤圣既已饮，
何必求神仙。
三杯通大道，
一斗合自然。
但得酒中趣，
勿为醒者传。

No. 2

If Heaven were not fond of wine,
There would be no Wine Star divine.
If the world were not fond of wine,
There would be no Wine Spring, so fine.
Since Heaven and earth both love wine,
I'm not shamed with Bacchus, God mine.
Limpid wine is a saint, as told;
Turbid wine is a sage, well sold.
Since saints and sages all drink wine,
Why should I invite beings divine?
Three cups can lead to the great Way;

With one jar, in Nature you'll stay.
Out of wine I just have my fun
That's unknown to a sober one.

* Wine Star: In Chinese mythology, there is a god called Wine Star in the Heavens, who taught Eeti how to brew wine in about 2200 B.C.
* Wine Spring: Spring of Wine, a city called Chiuch'üan if transliterated, in the western part of today's Kansu Province, as is said to have possessed a natural fountain of wine. According to *Myths and Marvels* (Shen-e Ching), in the wilderness of West China, there gurgles a fountain of wine pure like jade, more than 3 meters in width and more than 10 meters in depth and, which can revive or rejuvenate a drinker to eternal life. And a folklore source says in the Western Han dynasty, Swift Huo (140 B.C.- 117 B.C.) put his wine into the spring so that there would be an adequate supply for a celebration party after their defeating a Hun invasion, hence the name.
* Bacchus: the god of wine and revelry.
* the great Way: the Word, the most important notion in Chinese culture, which may be identified with the Word or the Logos in Western philosophy or cosmology.

其 三

三月咸阳城，
千花昼如锦。
谁能春独愁，
对此径须饮。
穷通与修短，
造化夙所禀。
一樽齐死生，
万事固难审。
醉后失天地，
兀然就孤枕。
不知有吾身，
此乐最为甚。

No. 3

The third moon sees in Allshine Town
All blossoms burst, red, white and pink.
But who knows that I'm feeling down?
Why don't you come and have a drink?
Rich or poor, long or short, you'll find,
All's made by Nature, so designed.
Death and life are in the same cup;
Of nothing we're sure, down or up.
I lose Heaven and earth when drunk
And throw all myself to the bunk.
Drunk, of myself I'm not aware;
Where to find such fun, here or there?

* Allshine: Hsienyang if transliterated, the capital of the Ch'in Empire. It is so called because all its rivers and mountains could get sunshine from all around. It was built in 350 B.C. and Ch'in moved its capital here the next year from Oakshine (Liyang).

其 四

穷愁千万端，
美酒三百杯。
愁多酒虽少，
酒倾愁不来。
所以知酒圣，
酒酣心自开。
辞粟卧首阳，
屡空饥颜回。
当代不乐饮，
虚名安用哉。
蟹螯即金液，
糟丘是蓬莱。
且须饮美酒，
乘月醉高台。

No. 4

A thousand woes do me entwine;
I have three hundred cups of wine.
Woes are many, wine a bit sum;
When I drink up, woes do not come.
So the saints of wine, as I know,
Once drinking, have all their cares go.
No rice, on Firstshine Bowone lay;
Do cheer, Hui Yan would hungry stay.
If you don't like wine or drink in time,
What's the use of fame to your prime?
Crabs can be the best food you'll find;

Knolls can be Fairylands combined.
Let's go uphill and drink some wine;
Drunk we reel to see Luna shine.

* Firstshine: Mt. Firstshine, located in today's Weiyüan County. It is the highest of all mountains there, so it is the first to receive sunshine, hence the name, and it is famous because two princes from the State of Lonebamboo called Bowone and Straightthree died of starvation here for their rectitude.
* Bowone: a childe in the late Shang dynasty. As he failed to admonish King Martial of Chough, Bowone left King Chough and refused to take crops reaped under the reign of Chough. He lived on fungi on Mt. Firstshine and starved to death in the end.
* Hui Yan: Hui Yan (521 B.C.- 481 B.C.) or Yanhui, Confucius's most diligent student, one of Confucius's seventy-two well-established disciples, a thinker in the late Spring and Autumn period. Confucius once commended him like this: "What a man Yanhui is! With A bowl of meal, a kettle of water, He lives in a shabby hut. No one can tolerate such poverty, but Yanhui feels happy about it. What a man he is!"
* Fairyland: an ideal abode for immortals, sometimes thought of as being in the middle of East Sea, sometimes in the sky.
* Luna: the moon, a symbol of solitude or happy reunion in Chinese culture. It is the goddess of the moon and of months in Roman mythology, and in Chinese culture the imperial concubine of Lord Alarm (2480 B.C.- 2345 B.C.), one of five mythical emperors in prehistorical China.

春归终南山松龛旧隐

我来南山阳，
事事不异昔。
却寻溪中水，
还望岩下石。
蔷薇缘东窗，
女萝绕北壁。
别来能几日，
草木长数尺。
且复命酒樽，
独酌陶永夕。

Retiring to the Old Abode of Pine Shrine in the South Hill in Spring

I arrive south of the South Hill;
There is nothing that has changed here.
Where has water gone from the rill?
To find it, neath the stone I peer.
The rose to East Sill shows its sprays;
The vines sprawl on the northern wall.
Since I came, it's but a few days;
The plants have grown several feet tall.
Set the table and cups again;
Let's drink and all night drunk remain.

* the South Hill: also known as the South Mountains, Mt. Great One, Mt. Earthlungs,

the mountains south of Long Peace, a great stronghold of the capital of the T'ang Empire, towering in the middle of Ch'in Ridge and rolling about 100 kilometers. It is the birthplace of Wordist culture, Buddhist culture, Filial Piety culture, Longevity culture, Bellheads culture and Plutus culture and is praised as the Capital of Fairies, the crown of Heavenly Abode and the Promised Land of the World.

* rose: any of a genus of shrubs of the rose family, characteristically with prickly stems, alternate compound leaves, and five-parted, usually fragrant flowers of red, pink, white, yellow, etc, having many stamens. It is often used as a metaphor for beauty or love.

冬夜醉宿龙门觉起言志

醉来脱宝剑,
旅憩高堂眠。
中夜忽惊觉,
起立明灯前。
开轩聊直望,
晓雪河冰壮。
哀哀歌苦寒,
郁郁独惆怅。
傅说板筑臣,
李斯鹰犬人。
欻起匡社稷,
宁复长艰辛。
而我胡为者?
叹息龙门下。
富贵未可期,
殷忧向谁写?
去去泪满襟,
举声梁甫吟。
青云当自致,
何必求知音?

Putting Up for the Night at Dragongate When Drunk on a Winter Night and Expressing My Will When Waking Up

I take off my sword, drunk, so deep,

And rest in the hall, fast asleep
I sudd'nly wake up at midnight,
And rise to stand before the light.
I ope the window to look out;
The snow shrouds the river throughout.
To the bitter coldness I croon,
And sigh to myself, all alone.
Yüeh Fu was an earth ramming slave;
Ssu Li reared dogs and eagles brave.
If they rose to support the state,
They must have suffered hardship great.
What have I been doing here? Why?
In Dragongate I sigh and sigh.
Wealth and ranks one cannot ask for;
To whom can I my cares deplore?
Gone, gone I feel my tears drip down;
I sing *O Father Liang* to frown.
For gains on yourself you'd depend,
Why ask a friend to recommend?

* Dragongate: west of Loshine, famous for its Buddhist grottoes.
* Yüeh Fu: Master Joy literally, a noble minister of high reputation in the Shang dynasty. Historic records say that the King of Shang dreamed of a sage, and he sent people out to search for him and found Yüeh Fu.
* Ssu Li: Ssu Li (284 B.C. - 208 B.C.), a renowned statesman, litterateur and calligrapher, whose political ideas have had a profound impact on China and laid the foundation of China's political system for more than two thousand years. Before he went to Ch'in, Li was a hunter in hometown, Tsai Gate.
* dog: a domesticated carnivorous mammal (*Canis familiaris*), of worldwide distribution and many varities, noted for its adaptability and its devotion to man. The dog was domesticated in China at least 8,000 years ago and used as a hunter, as a poem in *The Book of Songs* says: "The dog bells clink and clink; / The hunter's handsome, a real pink."

* eagle: a diurnal bird of prey of the family *Accipitridae* of worldwide distribution, notable for keen sight and strong flight, usually trained as a hunter and praised as a hero in Chinese culture.
* *O Father Liang*: a folk tune used as an elegy.

寻山僧不遇作

石径入丹壑，
松门闭青苔。
闲阶有鸟迹，
禅室无人开。
窥窗见白拂，
挂壁生尘埃。
使我空叹息，
欲去仍裴回。
香云徧山起，
花雨从天来。
已有空乐好，
况闻青猿哀。
了然绝世事，
此地方悠哉！

Written When Failing to See the Monk

The stone path leads to the red dale;
The pine door shut, moss does prevail.
Birds cheep, steps not used any more;
The Zen room closed, closed is the door.
The window does a dust whisk see;
It's hung on the wall, where dust be.
I sigh o'er there and sigh in vain;
I would go but come back again.
Balmy clouds from the hills arise;

Petal rain falls down from the skies.
Dulcet music rings in the air;
And blue monkeys' cries I do hear.
Free from the dust world we should rest;
This place is nice, it is the best!

* pine door: door made of pine wood. The pine is any of a genus (*Pinus*) of evergreen trees of the pine family, a cone-bearing tree having bundles of two to five needle-shaped leaves growing in clusters, an important image in Chinese literature, a symbol of rectitude, longevity and so on.
* Zen room: the room in which Zen is practiced. Zen is a kind of performance of quietude in a form of meditation or contemplation. When the Sanskrit word jana was introduced to China, it was translated as Zan or Zen for this kind of practice. In the T'ang dynasty, educated Chinese were imbued with Zen, and many of them were associated with Zen monks and spent much time in Zen monasteries.
* monkey: any of a group of primates having elongate limbs, hands and feet adapted for grasping, and a highly developed nervous system, including marmosets, baboons, and macaques, but not the anthropoid apes, though monkeys and apes are used alternatively in Chinese.

过汪氏别业二首
In Wang's Villa, Two Poems

其 一

游山谁可游？
子明与浮丘。
叠岭碍河汉，
连峰横斗牛。
汪生面北阜，
池馆清且幽。
我来感意气，
捶炰列珍羞。
扫石待归月，
开池涨寒流。
酒酣益爽气，
为乐不知秋。

No. 1

Who'll climb a mountain with you, who?
But Sir Shine and Float Knoll, the two.
The peaks high the Milky Way bar;
The ridges line up with Bullfight Star.
Wang's villa faces the North Hill;
The pool and kiosk are calm and still.
So friendly and kind is my host,
Who prepares all food, stew and roast.
He cleans the path for Luna's glow;

　　　　And digs a pond for a cold flow.
　　　　Refreshed, we drink to our full fill;
　　　　With glee, we forget autumn chill.

* Sir Shine: an immortal. Sir Shine, fond of fishing, once caught a white dragon. He felt scared and released it. Later, Shine got a white fish with a prescription in its body. He found all the ingredients and took them as elixir. Three years later, the white dragon came to pick him up onto a hill.
* Float Knoll: an immortal who used to make elixir with Lord Yellow on Mt. Yellow.
* the Milky Way: the Silver River in Chinese mythology, a luminous band circling the heavens composed of stars and nebulae; the Galaxy.
* Luna: the moon, a symbol of solitude or happy reunions in Chinese culture.

其 二

畴昔未识君，
知君好贤才。
随山起馆宇，
凿石营池台。
星火五月中，
景风从南来。
数枝石榴发，
一丈荷花开。
恨不当此时，
相过醉金罍。
我行值木落，
月苦清猿哀。
永夜达五更，
吴歈送琼杯。
酒酣欲起舞，
四座歌相催。
日出远海明，
轩车且徘徊。
更游龙潭去，
枕石拂莓苔。

No. 2

I did not know you well before
But hearing talents you adore.
You built your villa, hills around,
With a kiosk, a pool and a mound.
In the fifth moon Fire burns to glow;

A summer wind from south does blow.
The pomegranate shoots a few sprays;
The lotus tall in full bloom sways.
Fly to your place now I would fain,
To drink a cup, one cup again.
Now I've come, leaves begin to fall;
To the moon dim, sad monkeys squall.
Until dawn the night we prolong,
Drinking and singing a Wu song.
So drunk, we will rise up to dance;
The song around does us enhance.
The sun gets up the shore afar,
And here linger our horse and car.
We'd tour Dragon Abyss so deep;
Off Pillow Stone green moss we sweep.

* Fire: a star, also known Big Fire, what is Antares in Western astronomy.
* pomegranate: an Asian and African tree of the *Punica granatum* family, about the size of an orange, having bright, scarlet, flame-like flowers and bearing fruit with a hard rind and subacid red pulp with many seeds, a symbol of fertility and good life in Chinese culture.
* Dragon Abyss: usually a deep pool or pond.
* Pillow Stone: An ancient Chinese hermit often used a piece of stone as his pillow.
* moss: a tiny, delicate green bryophytic plant growing on damp decaying wood, wet ground, humid rocks or trees, producing capsules which open by an operculum and contain spores. Under a poet's writing brush, it may arouse a poetic feeling or imagination.

待 酒 不 至

玉壶系青丝，
沽酒来何迟。
山花向我笑，
正好衔杯时。
晚酌东窗下，
流莺复在兹。
春风与醉客，
今日乃相宜。

Drinking till Late

A blue band tied to my jade pot,
I am late, carrying wine I bought.
Now I drink out of my cup while
The mountain blossoms to me smile.
I drink till late by the east pane,
When warblers come back once again.
The wind will with us drinkers stay;
It's the best time for both today.

* jade pot: a pot in good quality, crystally bright, a pot usually alluding to integrity or the purity of the holder's heart and sometimes referring to the pure world of immortality, where elixirs are concocted.

独　酌

春草如有意，
罗生玉堂阴。
东风吹愁来，
白发坐相侵。
独酌劝孤影，
闲歌面芳林。
长松尔何知，
萧瑟为谁吟。
手舞石上月，
膝横花间琴。
过此一壶外，
悠悠非我心。

Drinking Alone

If spring grass has feeling at all,
It'll spread out in the shady hall.
The east wind blows a touch of care
To me and into my gray hair.
I drink and my shadow persuade;
To the wood sing a serenade.
The tall pines, do you ever know,
Are soughing for someone like so?
The moon o'er stone I wave to please;
Mid blooms the lute is on my knees.
Beyond the pot, out of the brink,

> There's nothing I will do or think.

* pine: any of a genus (*Pinus*) of evergreen trees of the pine family, a cone-bearing tree having bundles of two to five needle-shaped leaves growing in clusters, an important image in Chinese literature, a symbol of rectitude, longevity and so on.
* the moon: the satellite of the earth, which gives off light at night, a symbol of solitude, purity or happy reunion in Chinese literature or culture, with at least two hundred names, like Shade Spirit (yinp'o), Jade Toad (yüch'an), Jade Mound (yaot'ai), Fair Lady (ts'anchüan), Jade Hare (yüt'u), White Hare (pait'u), Silver Hare (yint'u), Ice Hare (pingt'u), Gold Hare (chint'u), Hare Gleam (t'uhui), Laurel Soul (Kuip'o) and so on.

友 人 会 宿

涤荡千古愁，
留连百壶饮。
良宵宜清谈，
皓月未能寝。
醉来卧空山，
天地即衾枕。

Staying with My Friend One Night

I'd get rid of my age-old woe;
With five score pots of wine I go.
It's good for a free talk at night,
As I can't sleep neath the moon bright.
Awake, by the hill now I lie;
My bed's the earth, and quilt the sky.

* the moon: the planet of the earth, which appears at night and gives off shining silvery light, an image of purity and solitude as it is always alone.
* My bed's the earth, and quilt the sky: the life style of a hermit or immortal.

春日独酌二首

Drinking Alone on a Spring Day, Two Poems

其 一

东风扇淑气,
水木荣春晖。
白日照绿草,
落花散且飞。
孤云还空山,
众鸟各已归。
彼物皆有讬,
吾生独无依。
对此石上月,
长歌醉芳菲。

No. 1

The east wind a fair air does blow;
The watered plants have a spring hue.
The white sun makes the green grass bright;
The blossoms are dispersed in flight.
There to the hills comes back the cloud;
The birds have come back in a crowd.
They have something to depend on,
I've nowhere to lean, a stray one.
With Luna o'er stone face to face,

Now drunk, I sing to the bloom's grace.

* Luna: the moon, an important image in Chinese literature, with many cultural associations such as feminity, purity, loneliness, vicissitudes of life and so on.

其 二

我有紫霞想，
缅怀沧洲间。
且对一壶酒，
澹然万事闲。
横琴倚高松，
把酒望远山。
长空去鸟没，
落日孤云还。
但悲光景晚，
宿昔成秋颜。

No. 2

I would abide in clouds much higher

Or lakes and seas I do desire.

Standing in front of a wine pot,

Relieved of all, I'm the whole lot.

With the lute, I lean on the pine,

And gaze at the hills, holing wine.

From the broad sky, all birds have gone.

Lo, the lone clouds, the setting sun.

I sigh long: It's but afterglow,

With my withered face wet with woe.

* lute: a Chinese lute, a stringed musical instrument, usually placed on a table, played by plucking the strings with fingers or a plectrum.
* pine: any of a genus (*Pinus*) of evergreen trees of the pine family, a cone-bearing tree having bundles of two to five needle-shaped leaves growing in clusters, an important image in Chinese literature, a symbol of rectitude, longevity and so on.

金陵江上遇蓬池隐者

心爱名山游,
身随名山远。
罗浮麻姑台,
此去或未返。
遇君蓬池隐,
就我石上饭。
空言不成欢,
强笑惜日晚。
绿水向雁门,
黄云蔽龙山。
叹息两客鸟,
裴回吴越间。
共语一执手,
留连夜将久。
解我紫绮裘,
且换金陵酒。
酒来笑复歌,
兴酣乐事多。
水影弄月色,
清光奈愁何。
明晨挂帆席,
离恨满沧波。

Meeting Thistle Pond Hermit on the Goldhill River

My heart loves a mount with a fame;
My legs seek a hill with a name.
Goddess Mound with Mt. La Phu there
Is where I'll go and return ne'er.
I meet you, a hermit well known;
You ask me to dine at the stone.
An idle talk does not please one;
We laugh a mere laugh to the sun.
Blue water to Wild Geese Gate flows;
Clouds greet the Dragon Hill, so close.
The two passenger birds, I sigh,
Between Wu and Yüeh so oft fly.
Hand in hand, for so long we chat;
The night is long, so long like that.
I doff my fur with purple shine,
So that I can buy Gold Hill wine.
With wine now, we laugh and we sing;
Drinking to us much fun does bring.
The stream light fondles the moon's hue;
Their shining does invoke my rue.
We will set sail tomorrow morn;
So sad, the river blue looks worn.

* Goddess Mound: south of Mt. La Phu, with White Lotus Pool below.
* Mt. La Phu: an attractive mountain in Kuangtung, where Surge Ko, a hermit in the Chin dynasty, used to live in seclusion.

* Wild Geese Gate: Mt. Wild Geese Gate, 30 kilometers from Up One County, Rivercalm Prefecture, that is, today's Nanking.
* the Dragon Hill: 22.5 kilometers from Rivercalm County, in present-day Nanking.
* Wu and Yüeh: the State of Wu and the State of Yüeh, or the south of China in general.
* Gold Hill: referring to Nanking, one of the most well-known ancient cities in China, a strategic fort as a gateway to the sea, which has been the capital of Wu, Chin, and many other states or kingdoms, such as the six empires called Six Dynasties and has flourished immensely with increasing trade and travel.

月夜听卢子顺弹琴

闲夜坐明月，
幽人弹素琴。
忽闻悲风调，
宛若寒松吟。
白雪乱纤手，
绿水清虚心。
钟期久已没，
世上无知音。

Listening to Tseshun Lu Playing the Zither on a Moonlit Night

The night chill, I sit neath the moon,
Listening to his zither old.
Now plucked is *Sad Wind*, a sad tune,
As if a sough shakes the pines cold.
White Snow flows out of his deft hand;
Green Water does a void heart cool.
Tsech'i passed away from this land,
No one can be your knowing soul.

* zither: a simple form of a stringed instrument, having a flat sounding board and from thirty to forty strings that are played by plucking with a plectrum. Zither, together with chess, calligraphy and painting are four skills that a traditional literateur is expected to master.
* *Sad Wind*: a lyric in *Zither Scores*, a collection of Buddhist Songs.
* *White Snow*: an elegant high-brow tune in ancient times.

* *Green Water*: a lyric in *Zither Scores*, a collection of Buddhist Songs.
* Tsech'i: referring to Tsech'i Chung, a woodcutter good at appreciating his music. His friend Poya, a renowned literatus in the Spring and Autumn period, was good at playing the lute. When Poya played his lute, Chung could always tell what he was playing about. After Chung's death, Poya broke his instrument for there was no man in the world to appreciate his music.

清溪半夜闻笛

羌笛梅花引，
吴溪陇水情。
寒山秋浦月，
肠断玉关声。

Hearing a Flute Tune by the Wu Stream at Midnight

The Wintersweet, a Ch'iang flute tune
Stirs up my rue by the Wu Stream.
The cold hills, the riverside moon,
To have heard *Jade Pass* song they seem.

* *The Wintersweet*: a Han Conservatoire flute tune.
* Ch'iang: a nationality living in the west of China, having the same origin as Chinese.
* the Wu Stream: a stream in a southern area of China.
* the moon: the planet of the earth, which appears at night and gives off shining silvery light, an image of purity, solitude and nostalgia as it is always alone.
* *Jade Pass*: a nostalgic story tracing back to Ts'ao Pan who garrisoned the border for 31 years and wished he could go back through Jade Pass alive.

日夕山中忽然有怀

久卧青山云，
遂为青山客。
山深云更好，
赏弄终日夕。
月衔楼间峰，
泉漱阶下石。
素心自此得，
真趣非外借。
鼯啼桂方秋，
风灭籁归寂。
缅思洪崖术，
欲往沧海隔。
云车来何迟，
抚几空叹息。

Inspired in the Hills at Dusk

For long in the green hills I rest,
So I become the green hills' guest.
In the hills deep, e'en clouds are great;
We enjoy each other till late.
Between tower and peaks, Luna glows;
Along the step stone, the spring flows.
Serene quietude you can behold;
Real pleasure can hardly be told.
A squirrel stirs the laurel chill;

When wind is gone, all's calm and still.
I'd learn the Word from Lord Cliff,
But barred by the blue, I've no skiff.
Why doesn't Cloud Cart come, o why?
I stroke the table while I sigh.

* laurel: an evergreen shrub with aromatic, lance-shaped leaves, yellowish flowers, and succulent, cherry-like fruit, a symbol of glory usually in the form of a crown or wreath of laurel to indicate honor or high merit, especially when one had passed Grand Test in ancient China. In Chinese mythology, there is a laurel tree on the moon, and it would never fall even though Kang Wu has kept cutting it.
* the Word: referring to Tao if transliterated, the most significant and profoundest concept in Chinese philosophy. According to Laocius's *The Word and the World*: "The Word is void, but its use is infinite. O deep! It seems to be the root of all things."
* Lord Cliff: an immortal.
* skiff: a light rowboat for fishing or lotus-picking and so on; formerly a sailing vessel.
* Cloud Cart: borrowed from a line of Lord Way's poem *Exhalation*, that is, Cloud Cart through the air.

夏 日 山 中

懒摇白羽扇，
裸袒青林中。
脱巾挂石壁，
露顶洒松风。

In the Hills on a Summer's Day

To flap my plumed fan I've no mood;
I, naked, lie in the green wood.
My scarf doffed hung on the cliff bare,
A wind thru pines blows o'er my hair.

* plumed fan: an image of the plumed fan used by Bright Chuke, the wise premier of the Kingdom of Shu.
* pine: any of a genus (*Pinus*) of evergreen trees of the pine family, a cone-bearing tree having bundles of two to five needle-shaped leaves growing in clusters, an important image in Chinese literature, a symbol of rectitude, longevity and so on.

山中与幽人对酌

两人对酌山花开，
一杯一杯复一杯。
我醉欲眠卿且去，
明朝有意抱琴来。

Drinking with a Hermit 'mid Mountain Blooms

'Mid blooms we drink, he to me, I to him,
One cup full and one more cup to the brim.
Now drunk, I'll have a good sleep. You may go.
Come tomorrow, and bring your lute with you.

* Now drunk, I'll have a good sleep. You may go: a quotation from Ch'ien T'ao, i.e. Poolbright T'ao.
* lute: a Chinese lute, a stringed musical instrument, usually placed on a table, played by plucking the strings with fingers or a plectrum.

春日醉起言志

处世若大梦，
胡为劳其生？
所以终日醉，
颓然卧前楹。
觉来盼庭前，
一鸟花间鸣。
借问此何时？
春风语流莺。
感之欲叹息，
对酒还自倾。
浩歌待明月，
曲尽已忘情。

Standing Up to Express Myself While Drunk

Life's like a dream, all in it drunk;
Why should we toil all life, o why?
All day long in good wine I'm sunk;
Like a log, in the hall I lie.
Awake, I look out of the hall;
A bird amid the blooms does cheep.
What time is it? Puzzled, I call.
At the birds a spring wind does peep.
To this sight I heave a long sigh,
And drink alone to drain my cup.

I invite the moon from the sky
To sing so that we both cheer up.

* I invite the moon from the sky: This personification is often used in Chinese poetry. In another poem Pai Li says:"My cup raised, I invite the moon, / With my shadow, three for the boon."

庐山东林寺夜怀

我寻青莲宇，
独往谢城阙。
霜清东林钟，
水白虎溪月。
天香生虚空，
天乐鸣不歇。
宴坐寂不动，
大千入毫发。
湛然冥真心，
旷劫断出没。

A Night in Eastwood Temple on Mt. Lodge

I go look for Green Lotus Hall,
So departing from the town wall.
The bell from Eastwood tolls frost bright;
The moon shines the Tiger Stream white.
Celestial balm flows from atop;
Heavenly bliss rings without stop.
In Nirvana I seem to sit;
The whole world's in my hair, a bit.
In absolute calm my heart be,
Of all banes and disasters free.

* Eastwood Temple: located at the foot of Mt. Lodge, built in A.D. 384, the Eastern Chin dynasty.

* Mt. Lodge: a famous mountain with historic, cultural and religious attractions, an especially sacred place to Wordists, about 5,000 feet high, in present-day Chianghsi Province.
* Green Lotus Hall: referring to Celestial Buddhist Palace or a Buddhist mansion.
* the Tiger Stream: probably the big stream out of Eastwood Temple.
* Nirvana: the attainment of complete freedom from all mental, emotional and psychic tension.

寻雍尊师隐居

群峭碧摩天，
逍遥不记年。
拨云寻古道，
倚石听流泉。
花暖青牛卧，
松高白鹤眠。
语来江色暮，
独自下寒烟。

Looking for Master Reverent in Hiding

It seems the peaks would the sky climb;
There above, we need not use time.
Clouds doffed, an old path I look for;
Rock near, I hark to the spring pour.
In warm blooms a black ox does lie;
A white crane dwells a pine twig high.
We, talking, see dusk the stream fold,
So I go downhill in haze cold.

* a black ox: allusion to Laocius, who rode his black ox away to the west and never returned.
* crane: one of a family of large, long-necked, long-legged, heronlike birds allied to the rails, a symbol of integrity and longevity in Chinese culture, only second to the phoenix in cultural importance.

与史郎中钦听黄鹤楼上吹笛

一为迁客去长沙,
西望长安不见家。
黄鹤楼中吹玉笛,
江城五月落梅花。

Listening to a Flute Play with Shih, the Royal Guard, in Yellow Crane Tower

To Long Sand I am exiled, so depressed;
To the court that I've lost I now look west.
In Yellow Crane Tower there is a flute play;
Wintersweet blooms fall in the town in May.

* Yellow Crane Tower: a famous tower built by Wu in A.D. 223, located on the top of Mt. Snake, overlooking the Long River, one of the three historical attractions (the other two being Shine River Pavillion and the Old Lute Platform) of today's Wuhan, Hupei Province.
* Long Sand: Ch'angsha if transliterated, the capital city of present-day Hunan Province.
* wintersweet: Armeniaca mume Sieb in latin, a plant or shrub about 4 to 10 meters tall, bursting into bloom in the coldest of winter to herald spring with small yellow or red flowers giving off thick fragrance. It is a symbol of elegance, solitude and pride in Chinese culture for its blossoming and fragrance in the coldest season while all other plants are still dry, bare, and devoid of vitality. It belongs in "Four Gentlemen", the other three being the orchid, bamboo and chrysanthemum, and one of the "Three Cold Weather Friends", the other two being the pine and bamboo.

对　　酒

劝君莫拒杯，
春风笑人来。
桃李如旧识，
倾花向我开。
流莺啼碧树，
明月窥金罍。
昨日朱颜子，
今日白发催。
棘生石虎殿，
鹿走姑苏台。
自古帝王宅，
城阙闭黄埃。
君若不饮酒，
昔人安在哉。

Drinking Wine with a Friend

I pray, do not the cup refuse;
The spring wind, smiling, to us flows.
The peach trees are like friends we know;
To us all their bright blossoms blow.
The warblers in the trees cheer up;
The bright moon does peer at my cup.
Yesterday, your cheeks seemed to ray,
And today, you grow but hair gray.
In Stone Tiger Hall brambles grow;

From Kusu Mound deer and stags go.
The broad palaces in the past
Are veiled in dust, by dust harassed.
Now if you do not drink much wine,
E'en ancestors do not feel fine.

* peach: any of the plant (*Prunus Percica*), bearing a fleshy, juicy, edible drupe, cultivated in many varieties in temperate zones considered sacred in China, often used as a metaphor for a young woman, as a section of a poem in *The Book of Songs* reads: "The peach twigs sway, / Ablaze the flower; / Now she's married away, / Befitting her new bower."
* the moon: the celestial body that revolves around the earth from west to east as a satellite, which appears at night and gives off shining silvery light, a partner with one who is alone at night.
* Kusu Mound: a palace King Futs'ai (cir. 528 B.C.- 473 B.C.) of the State of Wu built for his imperial concubine West Maid, one of the most beautiful women in Chinese history.
* deer and stags: ruminants (family *Cervidae*), having deciduous antlers, stags being the male and doe the female. A deer is usually a symbol of imperial power as it is often a target of pursuit.

醉题王汉阳厅

我似鹧鸪鸟，
南迁懒北飞。
时寻汉阳令，
取醉月中归。

Writing an Inscription for Magistrate Wang's Hall

Very much like a partridge, I
Have come south and will not north fly.
For you, magistrate, I oft come,
And drunk, in moonlight I go home.

* very much like a partridge, I: an allusion to Hua Chang's *Notes on Fowls*—a partridge like a female pheasant flies south, not turning back north.
* partridge: a kind of small, plump-bodied gallinaceous game bird, having white spots on the chest, a symbol of lovesickness in Chinese culture, as it utters a cry sounding like: "bro-bro, no-go-go".

嘲王历阳不肯饮酒

地白风色寒,
雪花大如手。
笑杀陶渊明,
不饮杯中酒。
浪抚一张琴,
虚栽五株柳。
空负头上巾,
吾于尔何有?

Laughing at Wang, Magistrate of Leeshine, Who Does Not Drink Wine

The wind blows cold, white all the land;
A snowflake's as big as a hand.
Poolbright T'ao will with laughter burst,
If you do not drink, do not thirst.
No use playing the lute amain,
And you planted willows in vain.
You let down your scarf on your hair;
Am I something to you, ne'er, e'er?

* Leeshine: an ancient town of strategic importance, in present-day Ho County, Anhui Province. It is the hub of roads and waterways between the Long River and the Huai River, with a rich historic legacy such as Soul Shrine of Overlord Yü Hsiang and Yün Wu's Lane, Yarn Washer's Shrine and so on.
* Poolbright: Ch'ien T'ao (A.D. 352 – A.D. 427) or Yüanming Tao if transliterated, a verse writer, poet, and litterateur in the Chin dynasty, and the founder of Chinese

idyllism. He was once the magistrate of P'engtse, but he resigned four times to live in reclusion. All in all, he can be remembered as a complex figure and a poet of complex poems, as has been termed by J. P. Seaton.

独坐敬亭山

众鸟高飞尽，
孤云独去闲。
相看两不厌，
只有敬亭山。

Sitting Alone Before Mt. Chingt'ing

All birds have away on high;
The lonely cloud at ease drifts by.
Eye to eye, neither has been bored;
Mt. Chingt'ing only is adored.

* Mt. Chingt'ing: an offset of Mt. Yellow, consisting of 60 peaks, rolling more than three miles and 317 meters above sea level, a mountain with many literary legacies, located near Hsuan, Anhui Province.

自　遣

对酒不觉暝，
落花盈我衣。
醉起步溪月，
鸟还人亦稀。

Drinking to Myself

While I drink, it's dark all too soon;
To my clothes fallen blossoms blow.
Drunk, I stroll the stream neath the moon;
Birds are gone and people are few.

* I stroll the stream neath the moon: This line suggests a fusion of the three—I, the stream and the moon, befitting the poet's romance.
* the moon: the planet of the earth, which gives off shining silvery light at night, an image of purity and solitude, and a companion with one who is alone.

访戴天山道士不遇

犬吠水声中，
桃花带雨浓。
树深时见鹿，
溪午不闻钟。
野竹分青霭，
飞泉挂碧峰。
无人知所去，
愁倚两三松。

Failing to See the Monk on Mt. Skywear

The water mirrors a dog's bay;
The peach blossoms carry thick dew.
In the deep woods, deer pass or stay;
The stream at noon hears no toll due.
The wild bamboo divides the brume;
The waterfalls down the peak fly.
No one knows where he's gone to roam;
Against two or three pines I sigh.

* Mt. Skywear: located in Riveroil (Chiangyu), Pai Li's hometown. On the mountain is All begun Temple, where Pai Li once studied.
* dog: a domesticated carnivorous mammal (*Canis familiaris*), of worldwide distribution and many varities, noted for its adaptability and its devotion to man. The dog was domesticated in China at least 8,000 years ago and was often used as a hunter, as a poem in *The Book of Songs* says: "The dog bells clink and clink; / The hunter's handsome, a real pink."

* peach: any of the plant (*Prunus Percica*), bearing a fleshy, juicy, edible drupe, cultivated in many varieties in temperate zones considered sacred in China, often used as a metaphor for a young woman, as a section of a poem in *The Book of Songs* reads: The peach twigs sway, / Ablaze the flower; / Now she's married away, / Befitting her new bower.
* deer: a ruminant (family *Cervidae*), having deciduous antlers, usually in the male only, as the moose, elk, and reindeer. Deer are closely related to Chinese life. Deer hide is a precious gift, especially presented to a female and a deer is usually a symbol of imperial power as it is often a target of pursuit.
* bamboo: a tall, tree-like or shrubby grass in tropical and semi-tropical regions, a symbol of integrity and altitude, one of the four most important images in Chinese literature, which are wintersweet, orchid, bamboo and chrysanthemum.

秋日与张少府、楚城韦公藏书高斋作

日下空庭暮,
城荒古迹馀。
地形连海尽,
天影落江虚。
旧赏人虽隔,
新知乐未疏。
彩云思作赋,
丹壁间藏书。
楂拥随流叶,
萍开出水鱼。
夕来秋兴满,
回首意何如?

Staying with Sheriff Chang and Wei, Magistrate of Ch'u, in the Latter's Library on an Autumn Day

The sun sunk, the yard lies in vain;
The town now waste, relics remain.
The terrain rolls to the sea shore;
Shown in the river, clouds still soar.
Tho my old friends are far away,
With new ones I happily stay.
Seeing clouds, we let our verse pour;
In the red wall, books we can store.
The raft floats with leaves all about;

> From duckweed a few fish jump out.
> At dusk, autumn hues still appeal;
> When looking back, how do you feel?

* raft: a float of logs, planks etc., fastened together for transportation by water. The sheepskin bag raft is a special craft made of 14 to 600 hundred sheepskin bags, varying according to the size of the raft, mainly used on the part of the Yellow River that flows through Lanchow in Kansu Province.
* duckweed: any of several small, disk-shaped, floating aquatic plants common in streams and ponds.

秋夜独坐怀故山

小隐慕安石,
远游学屈平。
天书访江海。
云卧起咸京。
入侍瑶池宴,
出陪玉辇行。
夸胡新赋作,
谏猎短书成。
但奉紫霄顾,
非邀青史名。
庄周空说剑,
墨翟耻论兵。
拙薄遂疏绝,
归闲事耦耕。
顾无苍生望,
空爱紫芝荣。
寥落暝霞色,
微茫旧壑情。
秋山绿萝月,
今夕为谁明?

Reminiscing the Old Hill When Sitting Alone on an Autumn Night

Retired a bit, Hsieh I admire;
To go far, of Ch'ü I deem higher

Go to the sea! Go to the skies;
E'en clouds from the capital rise.
At feast I serve the Lord with heart;
Out, I accompany His cart.
I write to praise the hunting Huns;
My remonstrances are short ones.
A purple cloud I now would ride,
Leaving all ranks or fame aside.
No talk about swords with Sir Lush;
Mentioning war to Ink, you'd blush.
Away from flunkies I go now;
With leisure, farmland I will plough.
Helpless to the world I remain;
I've loved Ganoderma in vain.
The dispersed clouds the haze does veil,
And hazed is my love for the dale.
The moon o'er the autumn hill vine,
This even, for whom does it shine?

* Hsieh: referring to An Hsieh (A.D. 320 – A.D. 385), a statesman and renowned scholar in the Eastern Chin dynasty. When Hsieh was playing chess with his friend, a letter came but Hsieh continued to play chess without response after reading it. His guest asked him about the letter, he answered in calmness: "My son has defeated the enemy." Not until Hsieh went back into his room did he realize that he was too happy to find his shoes had already broken.
* Sir Lush: Sir Lush (369 B.C.– 286 B.C.), a great thinker, philosopher and litterateur in the Warring States period. As a principal founder of Wordism, Sir Lush enjoys as high a reputation as Laocius.
* Ink: Sir Ink (cir. 476 B.C.– 390 B.C.), a great thinker and the founder of Inkism (usually known as Mohism), a proponent of the doctrine of universal love (fraternity) and non-aggression.
* Ganoderma: *Ganoderma Lucidum Karst* in Latin, a grass with an umbrella top, a pore fungus, used as medicine and tonic in China.

忆崔郎中宗之游南阳遗吾孔子琴抚之潸然感旧

昔在南阳城，
唯餐独山蕨。
忆与崔宗之，
白水弄素月。
时过菊潭上，
纵酒无休歇。
泛此黄金花，
颓然清歌发。
一朝摧玉树，
生死殊飘忽。
留我孔子琴，
琴存人已没。
谁传广陵散，
但哭邙山骨。
泉户何时明，
长归狐兔窟。

Reminiscing Tsungchih Ts'ui, the Royal Guard, Touring Southshine, and Crying over the Lute He Left to Me

Then in Southshine, facing the sun;
Only on wild fern did I dine.
I reminisce Ts'ui, my beloved one,
With whom I splashed to the moon shine.

Once Chrysanthemum Pool we passed,
Where we drank and our glee did last.
The yellow blossoms were stirred now,
And our song was blown by a sough.
The emerald tree fell to the blast;
Its life was down to the vale cast.
His Con House lute was left to me,
But the lute player ceased to be.
Who'll pass the Broadridge tune around?
We can but cry out to Mang Mound.
When can his tomb be brightened, when?
There foxes or hares build their den.

* Tsungchih Ts'ui: a high T'ang official, a royal guard, and ennobled as Count of Ch'i, the fourth of the Eight Immortals of the Wine Cup (Eight Wine Cups for short), so described by Fu Tu: "The fourth Immortal a handsome youth be, / His cup raised to the sky, eyes filled with glee, / Pure like a fairy draught from a jade tree."
* Southshine: an alternative name for South Town, which had nurtured the Five Sages of Southshine—Great Grand, Sage of Wisdom in the Shang and Chough dynasties, Li Fan (536 B.C.- 448 B.C.), Sage of Commerce in the Spring and Autumn period, Heng Chang (A.D. 78 - A.D. 139), Sage of Science in the Eastern Han dynasty, Chungching Chang, Sage of Medicine in the Eastern Han dynasty, and Bright Chuke (A.D. 181 - A.D. 234), Sage of Strategy in the Eastern Han dynasty.
* fern: any of a widely distributed class of flowerless, seedless pteridophytic plants, having roots and stems and feathery leaves (fronds) which carry the reproductive spores in clusters of sporangia called sori. Its young stems and root starch are table delicacies to Chinese now as well as in the past.
* Chrysanthemum Pool: a pool caused by a stream flowing from Mt. Stone Horse northwest of Southshine Town, where chrysanthemums were especially fragrant and dozens of households drinking the water there could mostly live more than one hundred years.
* Broadridge tune: one of the Ten Songs in Chinese history.
* Mang Mound: the place where Ts'ui was buried.
* fox: a burrowing canine mammal (genus *Vulpes*) having a long pointed muzzle and a

long bushy tail, commonly reddish-brown in color, characterized by its cunning.
* hare: a rodent (genus *Lepus*) with cleft upper lip, long ears, and long hind legs, characterized by its timidity and swiftness, habitating woodland, farmland or grassland.

忆东山二首

Recollection of the East Hills, Two Poems

其 一

不向东山久，
蔷薇几度花。
白云还自散，
明月落谁家。

No. 1

The East Hills I've not seen for long;
The roses bloom to die, and die to bloom.
The clouds by themselves part or throng;
Where has Luna dropped, to whose home?

* the East Hills: located in today's Shaohsing, Chechiang Province, the hills where An Hsieh (A.D. 320 – A.D. 385), a statesman and litterateur with high reputation, lived with ease and kept declining official positions until he was in his forties. It is often used as a metaphor for reclusion.
* rose: any of a genus of shrubs of the rose family, characteristically with prickly stems, alternate compound leaves, and five-parted, usually fragrant flowers of red, pink, white, yellow, etc, having many stamens. It is often used as a metaphor for beauty or love.
* Luna: Godess of the Moon in Roman mythology; the moon, a symbol of solitude, nostalgia and the purity of many other things in Chinese culture.

其 二

我今携谢妓，
长啸绝人群。
欲报东山客，
开关扫白云。

No. 2

Now I've a courtesan with me,
So with a hail, I'll leave the crowd.
Guests in the East Hills, I'll tell thee,
Open the pass! Sweep off the cloud!

* courtesan: professional woman singer or lutenist, like *geisha* in Japan.
* the East Hills: located in Shaohsing, where General An Hsieh (A.D. 320 – A.D. 385) retreated for his country life. "Rising again from the East Hills" is a Chinese idiom that alludes to An Hsieh's rise to defeat the invasion of Chien Fu's army after years of country life as a recluse.

望 月 有 怀

清泉映疏松，
不知几千古。
寒月摇清波，
流光入窗户。
对此空长吟，
思君意何深。
无因见安道，
兴尽愁人心。

Stirred When Looking at the Moon

The spring mirrors the sparse-leafed pines,
Which may have lived thousands of years.
The chill moon to the ripples shines,
Her gleam into the window peers.
To this, I could but in vain sigh,
How intense I feel about you!
Why can't I see you here, o why?
My heart is overfilled with rue.

* the chill moon: an image of loneliness and nostalgia in Chinese literature. The moon accompanies our poet all his life. He drinks to the moon, his cup, his shadow and the moon making a party of three; he raises his head to the moon and thinks of his hometown; he reaches for the moon while drunk and gets drowned before ascending the sky, astride a whale.

对酒忆贺监二首(并序)

Drinking and Reminiscing Mr. Ho, Two Poems with an Introduction

太子宾客贺公,于长安紫极宫一见余,呼余为"谪仙人",因解金龟换酒为乐。殁后对酒,怅然有怀,而作是诗。

When Mr. Ho, Crown Prince's Guest, saw me in Purple Palace in Long Peace, he, exclaiming, addressed me as Exiled Saint and exchanged his gold turtle for wine. Now he is dead, I drink sadly, hence the two poems.

其 一

四明有狂客,
风流贺季真。
长安一相见,
呼我谪仙人。
昔好杯中物,
翻为松下尘。
金龟换酒处,
却忆泪沾巾。

No. 1

There was a mad man at Four Bright,
A talent brilliant, known to all.
When in Long Peace, he, at first sight,
Cheered and did me Exiled Saint call.
Our cups with love we used to hold;

　　　　Now you are dust neath the pine tree.
　　　　For wine you exchanged Turtle gold,
　　　　Which sometimes stirs up tears in me.

* Mr. Ho: Chihchang Ho (A.D. 659 - A.D. 744), styled Truth, and dubbed Mad Man at Four Bright, one of the Eight Wine Cups, a jovial courtier, renowned poet and calligrapher in the T'ang dynasty, who acclaimed Pai Li as Exiled Immortal to the public and introduced him to Emperor Deepsire.
* Purple Palace: name of a palace in Long Peace.
* a mad man: referring to Chihchang Ho, alias Mad Man.
* Four Bright: Mt. Four Bright, a mountain in today's Chechiang Province, standing opposite to Mt. Heaven Terrace.
* Long Peace: Ch'ang'an if transliterated, the capital of the T'ang Empire, present-day Hsi'an, which is West Peace literally. The other or secondary capital of T'ang was Loshine.

其 二

狂客归四明，
山阴道士迎。
敕赐镜湖水，
为君台沼荣。
人亡余故宅，
空有荷花生。
念此杳如梦，
凄然伤我情。

No. 2

Mad Man went back to Four Bright then,
So welcome by the Wordist men.
The Lord granted them a clear lake
So that a good tour they could make.
When one dies his estates remain;
Lotus blossoms burst there in vain.
Dream-like, life is out of control;
The mournfulness does grieve my soul.

* Mad Man: Chihchang Ho's alias.
* Four Bright: a mountain in Chechiang Province, standing opposite to Mt. Heaven, so named because it looks bright from all directions.
* Wordist: one who believes in and practices the Word, the ultimate being in the universe. In the T'ang dynasty, an age of proselytism, while Confucianism remained the guiding principle of state and social morality, Wordism had gathered an incrustation of mythology and superstition and was fast winning a following of both the court and the common people. Laocius, the founder, was claimed by the reigning dynasty as its remote progenitor and was honored with an imperial title, Emperor Dark One.

重忆一首

欲向江东去，
定将谁举杯？
稽山无贺老，
却棹酒船回。

Reminiscing the Past

To East Land I will make my way;
With whom shall I drink and drink more?
From Mt. Summit, Ho's passed away,
So I turn back and ply my oar.

* East Land: the area east of the Long River. From Wuhu to Nanking, the Long River flows northeast, so the area east of the River is called East Land.
* Mt. Summit: referring to the K'uaichi Mountains in present-day Chechiang Province, where Worm convened a summit attended by vassal lords, hence the name.
* Chihchang Ho: Chihchang Ho (A.D. 659 – A.D. 744), Pai Li's friend, an imperial tutor, a jovial courtier, a renowned poet and calligraphist, one of the Eight Immortals of the Wine Cup. He acclaimed Pai Li as Fallen Immortal to the public and introduced him to Emperor Deepsire. At 86, he requested leave to return to his home in Shaohsing to become a Wordist monk and took flight to Heaven then and there.

春滞沅湘有怀山中

沅湘春色还，
风暖烟草绿。
古之伤心人，
于此肠断续。
予非怀沙客，
但美采菱曲。
所愿归东山，
寸心于此足。

Feeling Touched in the Hills When Kept at Bay in the Yüan-Hsiang Area in Spring

To the Yüan-Hsiang area spring's back;
The wind warms the grass in mist green.
Since ancient times, mourners, alack,
Have all wept here, so sad, so keen.
I'm not Yüan Ch'ü drowned with a stone
But love *Water Chestnut* so much.
I'd retire to the East Hills soon,
And I'll smile, contented as such.

* the Yüan-Hsiang area: an alternative name for Yüehchow.
* Yüan Ch'ü: Yüan Ch'ü (340 B.C.- 278 B.C.), a great patriotic poet and official of Ch'u, who threw himself into the Milo River, so aggrieved at his broken state.
* *Water Chestnut*: a folk song. When gathering water chestnuts, gatherers usually sang such a song.
* the East Hills: located in today's Shaohsing, Chechiang Province, the hills where An

Hsieh (A.D. 320 - A.D. 385), a statesman and litterateur with high reputation, lived with ease and kept declining official positions until he was in his forties. It is often used as a metaphor for reclusion.

落日忆山中

雨后烟景绿，
晴天散馀霞。
东风随春归，
发我枝上花。
花落时欲暮，
见此令人嗟。
愿游名山去，
学道飞丹砂。

Reminiscing the Hills at Sunset

It's mist and green after the rain;
The sky is clear and clouds remain.
The east wind and the spring both show
So that on the sprays blossoms blow.
The blooms will fall neath the murk sky;
At this dark scene one can but sigh.
I'll tour the famous hills afar
To learn how to smelt cinnabar.

* cinnabar: a crystallized red mercuric sulfide, HgS, the chief ore of mercury, the raw mineral material for elixir in Wordist alchemy.

忆秋浦桃花旧游,时窜夜郎

桃花春水生,
白石今出没。
摇荡女萝枝,
半挂青天月。
不知旧行径,
初拳几枝蕨。
三载夜郎还,
于兹炼金骨。

Reminiscing My Tour in Autumn Shore While Exiled to Nightboy

As peach blooms blow, spring waters surge;
The white stone in the stream submerge.
The dodder trailers sway to fly;
The moon hangs half way from the sky.
In the usual path there, I doubt
If fernworts as big as fists sprout.
In Nightboy for three years I've stayed;
Now back, I'll learn how cure-all's made.

* Autumn Shore: southwest of today's Kuich'ih County, Anhui Province, rich in silver and copper resources and teeming with fauna and flora.
* Nightboy: once the biggest kingdom founded by southern barbarians in the southwest existing from the Warring States period to the Han dynasty. When a Han envoy visited Nigthboy, the king asked: "Which is bigger, Nigthboy or Han?" This self-important question has been a laughing stock ever since. In 27 B.C., Nightboy was wiped out by

Han and was made a county.
* peach: any of the plant (*Prunus Percica*), bearing a fleshy, juicy, edible drupe, cultivated in many varieties in temperate zones considered sacred in China, often used as a metaphor for a young woman, as a section of a poem in *The Book of Songs* reads: "The peach twigs sway, / Ablaze the flower; / Now she's married away, / Befitting her new bower."
* dodder: a leafless twining herb of the genus *Cuscuta*, parasitic on several other plants to which it adheres by suckers, very harmful to crops like the soya bean.
* fernwort: any pteridophyte or fern, used as food when it is young and tender in China.